A
_____

CANDLELIGHT GEORGIAN SPECIAL

CANDLELIGHT REGENCIES

571 SENSIBLE CECILY, *Margaret Summerville*
572 DOUBLE FOLLY, *Marnie Ellingson*
573 POLLY, *Jennie Tremaine*
578 THE MISMATCHED LOVERS, *Anne Hillary*
579 UNWILLING BRIDE, *Marnie Ellingson*
580 INFAMOUS ISABELLE, *Margaret Summerville*
581 THE DAZZLED HEART, *Nina Pykare*
586 THE EDUCATION OF JOANNE, *Joan Vincent*
587 MOLLY, *Jennie Tremaine*
588 JESSICA WINDOM, *Marnie Ellingson*
589 THE ARDENT SUITOR, *Marian Lorraine*
593 THE RAKE'S COMPANION, *Regina Towers*
594 LADY INCOGNITA, *Nina Pykare*
595 A BOND OF HONOUR, *Joan Vincent*
596 GINNY, *Jennie Tremaine*
597 THE MARRIAGE AGREEMENT, *Margaret MacWilliams*
602 A COMPANION IN JOY, *Dorothy Mack*
603 MIDNIGHT SURRENDER, *Margaret Major Cleaves*
604 A SCHEME FOR LOVE, *Joan Vincent*
605 THE DANGER IN LOVING, *Helen Nuelle*
610 LOVE'S FOLLY, *Nina Pykare*
611 A WORTHY CHARADE, *Vivian Harris*
612 THE DUKE'S WARD, *Samantha Lester*
613 MANSION FOR A LADY, *Cilla Whitmore*
618 THE TWICE BOUGHT BRIDE, *Elinor Larkin*
619 THE MAGNIFICENT DUCHESS, *Sarah Stamford*
620 SARATOGA SEASON, *Margaret MacWilliams*
621 AN INTRIGUING INNOCENT, *Rebecca Ashley*
625 THE AVENGING MAID, *Janis Susan May*
626 THE HEART OF THE MATTER, *Diana Burke*
627 THE PAISLEY BUTTERFLY, *Phyllis Taylor Pianka*
631 MAKESHIFT MISTRESS, *Amanda Mack*
632 RESCUED BY LOVE, *Joan Vincent*
633 A MARRIAGEABLE ASSET, *Ruth Gerber*
637 THE BRASH AMERICAN, *Samantha Lester*
638 A SEASON OF SURPRISES, *Rebecca Ashley*
639 THE ENTERPRISING MINX, *Marian Lorraine*
643 A HARMLESS RUSE, *Alexandra Lord*
644 THE GYPSY HEIRESS, *Laura London*
645 THE INNOCENT HEART, *Nina Pykare*

THE CURIOUS ROGUE

Joan Vincent

A Candlelight Georgian Special

Published by
Dell Publishing Co., Inc.
1 Dag Hammarskjold Plaza
New York, New York 10017

Copyright © 1981 by Joan C. Wesolowsky

All rights reserved. No part of this book may be reproduced or transmitted in any form or by any means, electronic or mechanical, including photocopying, recording or by any information storage and retrieval system, without the written permission of the Publisher, except where permitted by law.

Dell ® TM 681510, Dell Publishing Co., Inc.

ISBN: 0-440-11186-2

Printed in the United States of America

First printing—April 1981

To Vince with love

THE
CURIOUS ROGUE

Chapter I

Billowing black clouds edged with slivers of white boiled about the moon, sporadically concealing its light. The sloop, having begun its journey on lightly tossed waves, was now plowing through ever larger whitecaps as it neared the chalk-white cliffs of the English coast. Having avoided the Channel patrols, which were either hastening to port or out to open sea to weather the gathering storm, the men aboard strove to deliver their cargo before finding a safe harbour, not an easy task in this danger-filled year of 1800.

On the sloop's deck, clad in oilskins, the men laboured to hold a steady course and cast worried glances towards shore. A twinkle of light, followed by a second and then a third, rewarded their vigilance. Smiles appeared on the grim-faced men. They eased the sails and maneuvered the sloop as close to shore as they dared in the rough seas.

Hooped barrels were hurriedly lowered over the sides into rowboats. With hushed tones and muffled oars, they were brought to shore.

"Best head for the safety of Folkestone's harbour,"

the tall dark man, his oilskin hood concealing his features, bade the captain.

"Aye, and ye'll be for a warmed bed," the weathered man grinned widely.

"Each of us has his own trial to bear," the other returned dryly, a hint of a smile slightly easing the fatigue on his features. "Farewell. A safe port be yours."

"And yers." Bidding each other farewell, they shook hands in mutual respect and friendship.

The dark man glanced about as the captain climbed into the rowboat. He noted that all the casks were gone from the sandy shore, borne away by silent-footed men. *The local gentry are assured their brandy for the season*, he thought. With a wave to his friend he turned and strode from the beach. Familiar with the lay of the land, he kept a steady pace up the rocky incline and into the tall grass and shrub-dotted terrain. With certainty he halted before a leaning pine and knelt, then unearthed a leather pouch. His oilskin was pulled off, rolled into a tight bundle, and exchanged for a heavy woolen cloak. This done, the pouch was put back and the sandy soil hurriedly pushed atop it.

The sharp report of a Brown Bess, carried from the beach by the wind, jerked the man's head about. "Excise men," he cursed, undoing the cloak and fastening it about him. Crouching low, he ran a short distance inland but realized that soldiers were closing in on the beach from all sides. Doubling back at a much slower pace, the cloaked figure edged his way to the officers' secreted mounts.

A long march and an equally lengthy wait in the chilling wind had dulled the only guard's sense of duty. He stood to one side, leaning sleepily upon his Brown Bess. One of the horses nickered and shied when the dark figure passed it. "Quiet now," the soldier reprimanded, not bothering to look around. He straightened as two shots sounded farther down the beach.

The stealthy figure slunk up behind the guard and brought his pistol down in a swift, decisive blow, rendering the man senseless. After untying all the mounts, keeping the best for himself, the man swung into the saddle and drove the horses down the beach towards the sounds of the rifle shots. Scuffling men separated and running figures dashed to safety as the horses galloped across the beach.

Three captured men gained their freedom in the pandemonium. Officers bellowed commands, demanding their steeds be captured and the prisoners retaken. The dark man driving the horses let loose a deep, mocking laugh as he passed them and disappeared into the darkness.

Heading across country, he made for a farm he had visited previously, certain a fresh mount could be obtained. To his consternation a loud voice commanded him to halt when he entered the farmyard. Reining his mount about, the man spurred away, a rifle ball whistling past his shoulder. His concern grew when thudding hooves bespoke pursuit. Fatigue fled. The challenge of evading his pursuers spurred the man on.

His last moments in France had been similarly spent. The French general Napoleon Bonaparte, recently freed from the bindings of the Directory by his coup d'etat, had ordered the arrest of any suspicious person, despite the fact that a majority of the people had approved his action by electing him First Consul. A certain M. Lanier had used this edict against the rider.

Stymied in his original intent, the cloaked figure headed for Folkestone. He had long ago made himself familiar with all of the coastal villages and towns for just such an emergency; he knew that several places for concealment existed if he could but put more distance between himself and those doggedly pursuing him. Taking a zigzag course, he slowly drew away from them.

Relief came with the sighting of twinkling lamplights in the distance. The first cold drops of rain fell as he gained the edge of the town. Passing through the tight lanes between the outer cottages, the man made for the more heavily populated section of Folkestone. He drew his cloak closer, to ward off the steadily increasing rain, and slowed his mount. The sound of an approaching carriage halted him in a lamplit area of the town. Vaulting from the saddle, he slapped the foam-covered steed on the rump, sending it down the street, then ducked into the shadows. A hurried examination assured him that his pistol was loaded and, more importantly, dry. He tucked it loosely in his waistband, readily available if the need arose.

May the gentleman within be foxed, asleep, or both, he thought as he waited for the carriage to pass. The sight of a lone, nodding guard beside the driver brought a smile to his face. Lunging from the shadows when the carriage came abreast, he pulled its door open and sprang inside, pulling his pistol free as he thudded into the far corner of the seat. To his surprise, the person he confronted was not a lone, sleeping gentleman.

A very angry, very feminine voice challenged him. "What do you mean by this? A robber is supposed to halt a coach, not vault into it like a madman. Besides, I have no money. You may just as well depart as you came."

The dim light of the streetlamps they passed provided glimpses of the occupant. Her smooth complexion and bright-eyed look bespoke a young woman, far too young for the white-edged spinster's cap showing beneath her modest bonnet. Her dress was conservative and for the most part covered by a serviceable pelisse, devoid of geegaws and furbelows.

"But madam, it is raining," he said lazily, waving his hand at the water-streaked windows of the carriage.

A quick indrawn breath at sight of the pistol in his hand was her only sign of dismay. The young woman relaxed, realizing that for some reason she did not feel threatened. She strained to get a better look at this high-handed rogue.

His cloak, held by a leather thong, had fallen off his shoulders when he had tumbled into the seat, revealing plain leather riding breeches and the knee-high jackboots common to men of the road. His full white shirt was open, baring a dark-haired, masculine chest. Feeling a blush rise to her cheeks at such an intimate sight, the young woman hurriedly raised her eyes to his face. Disappointment flared, for the hood of the cloak had remained up and she could not see his features plainly.

Wondering briefly at her composure in this situation, the young woman was distracted from her thoughts as the man gracefully crossed his legs, settling more comfortably against the squabs. His abrupt entry and the pistol still pointed at her were at odds with the air of gentility with which he carried himself.

The man grinned broadly upon observing her inspection of his person. Her colour mounted, and anger replaced curiosity. "If you are a gentleman, I bid you to depart as you came," she ordered.

"But a gentleman would never have entered as I," he answered, amused. He uncocked the pistol and laid it on the seat between them.

The young woman's anger was tempered by the reminder of the pistol, and she repressed the reprimand almost on her lips, repeating instead, "I have no money."

"But I do not mean to rob you." He leaned back in the seat. "Do you oft travel alone?"

The rogue means to stay, she decided, and turned her thoughts to a course of action. *Mayhaps I can distract his attention and gain hold of the weapon,* she thought, immediately putting the idea into action. "My uncle has taken ill and has summoned me to his home to nurse him. He is impatient in all things and demanded I come at once, sending his own coach for me. He lives near Ashford." She spoke in even, measured tones, her eyes moving from the man to the pistol and returning to him.

"It would be regrettable if you did not reach this uncle, or if some mishap occurred to you or perhaps to the driver or guard," he warned, surmising her intent.

Her hand was stayed by the implied threat. What manner of man was he? Curiosity pulsed strongly.

"We shall arrive at the tollgate soon," he said, glancing out the window. "Let your coachman pay the fee and pass on. No harm shall come to you or your uncle's servants. I wish only to ride a short distance."

"Is there no coach you can hire?" she asked icily.

"Ahhh, many." The man smiled. A sudden clamour ahead of the carriage caused him to take hold his pistol and cock it. The coach slowed and came to a halt before the tollgate. Lanterns bobbed about the windows as soldiers swarmed around the vehicle.

Looking inside, the sergeant gaped at the sight of a couple in fierce embrace, then burst into good-humoured laughter as the man within waved him to be gone while refusing to free his companion's lips. He slammed the door shut without a word and ordered the driver to pay the toll and go on. "I'd give a month's wages to be that man," he told the men beside him. "He'll have too brief a journey from the looks o' it. A willing wench on a night like this be what we all need."

Tossing rueful glances at the departing coach, the soldiers huddled against the rain, awaiting the next person or carriage. The smuggler they had followed had yet to be taken.

Inside the carriage the young woman stared at the man who still had his arm about her, although he had removed the pistol's point from her side. It had all

17

happened so quickly—the suddenness of his embrace, the pistol nudging her ribs, the feel of his lips . . . She allowed her thoughts to wander briefly over the pleasantness of the latter, then called herself to order. *Elizabeth Jeffries, the least you could have done is gone into a strong fit of hysterics. Any lady worthy of her genteelness would have fainted*, she admonished herself, a frown coming to her lips. *But then, I never faint*, she thought exasperatedly, meeting the man's quizzical gaze.

"I have held many women in my arms," he said, "but none ever thought to frown. Mayhaps you would like to swoon?" his deep voice offered. "Or scream?" he ended hopefully, perplexed and piqued to have elicited neither offense nor pleasure.

"It was . . . interesting," she offered, sensing he expected a comment from her.

A hint of affront entered his voice. "Interesting?"

"Was it to have been more?" Miss Jeffries questioned as he withdrew his arm.

"I am certainly relieved to hear it was not dull," he snorted.

"A strange man leaping into my carriage could never be dull . . . at least I don't think so. You are the first to have ever done it," Elizabeth returned, calmly straightening her bonnet.

Cursing silently at the darkness which prevented him from seeing her features, the intruder began to reassess his opinion of the young woman, for he prided himself on his perception. His life oft depended upon the correctness of such appraisals. The young woman beside him was a mull of contradictions. She dressed like any number of the young misses from the country abounding in London, yet traveled alone, which bespoke a note of daring or experience. Her lack of interest, response, or even repugnance at being kissed by a stranger prompted him to dismiss her as a lady of the "other sort," while her voice and words were far too strong for the usual delicate young miss. His pride tweaked, he couldn't decide whether to ignore her or learn more about her.

"Are you a smuggler?" the young woman asked, breaking the silence, her tone calm and even, as though asking if he would take tea.

"No," he answered gruffly, shaking his head in wonder at this unusual female, of a type he had never before encountered.

"A thief then?"

"I think not," he answered coldly.

"You would certainly be the one to know. Why, then, did you fear being discovered by the soldiers?"

"Young ladies should never speak to strangers," he told her quellingly. "If you must, would you not rather know of the latest style of dress in Paris?"

"Gowns are of no special inter . . . Paris? Are you an émigré?" A note of loathing had entered her voice.

"Do I sound like one?"

"No," she answered slowly, vexed not only because she felt he was laughing at her, but also because she felt an uncommon attraction to him.

"Why do you wear a spinster's cap beneath your bonnet?" he asked, giving way to his curiosity.

"Gentlemen do not ask such intimate questions of ladies," she retorted primly.

"But I thought we had agreed I was not a gentleman," he noted with mock seriousness. "Perhaps I need to prove it," he added leaning towards her.

"No," came swiftly. She drew back. "I permitted the first kiss merely to . . . to prevent you from shooting some innocent person," Miss Jeffries told him haughtily, sitting very rigid.

"Ahh, the nobility of womanhood." He sighed derisively, his earlier fatigue suddenly returning. He stifled a yawn as he settled back in his corner.

Sensing his exhaustion, the young woman pulled a squab from beside her. "Take this." She tossed it to him.

"For a rogue such as I?"

"Then be less high-handed and leave my presence soon," she snapped irritably, angry with herself for not reining in her impulse.

A deep chuckle answered her.

What has come over me, she thought, *thinking of this man's . . . this rogue's . . . comfort?*

Chapter II

The long silence, broken only by the wind-driven rain and the slosh of the team's hooves, convinced Miss Jeffries that the intruder had fallen asleep. For a time she questioned her strange lack of reaction to the evening's events but, drawing no logical conclusions, dismissed it as the result of her overabundance of curiosity and her totally unladylike mien. Her aunt Waddington had oft told her that her behaviour was far too insensitive for a lady and the likely cause of her lack of suitors.

Elizabeth sighed, wondering if there was a man in all England who did not want a simpering idiot for a wife. Her eyes turned to the man beside her. His wife certainly could not be missish if she was to survive his career, she thought, a smile coming to her lips. And, she noted mentally, that kiss *was* interesting, far better than Cousin Ralph's childish attempts six years past. He had been ghastly dreadful at the business. Now, Mr. Simpson was more learned in the art, but, alas, he was far too much the gentleman to attempt more than two, her thoughts continued in their unladylike trend. Her eyes turned to the figure beside her. *Yours was far better than either . . . I think. If only I could recall it with more certainty,* she ended, frowning at him. Elizabeth shook her head. *What manner of contemplation is this? You should be contriving to bring the man to justice. He must have committed some crime to fear the king's men.*

Carefully she reached out and felt across the seat for the pistol. *Now where has it gone?* she wondered, wishing it were not quite so dark. *Ahh, now I recall. He placed it in his belt. Do I dare?* she asked herself. *Why not?* her impetuous side prompted, and she moved slowly towards him.

Gingerly she felt for the edge of his cloak on the seat, found it, moved slowly up, and halted as her hand touched the cold steel of the pistol. Her heart lurched as his hand closed on hers.

"I . . . I thought it might be making you . . . uncomfortable," she blurted, trying to draw her hand back.

"Your consideration touches me greatly," he replied lightly, keeping his hold. "Tell me, what would you have done had you managed to get hold of it?"

"My . . . my uncle is a magistrate for Ashford. I would . . . I would have turned you over to him," she answered, refusing to be cowed.

"On what charge?"

"Oh, would it matter? There are probably many."

"What a cruel thing to do," he tisked sadly, "driving a sick man from his bed for your personal vengeance."

"There is nothing personal about this, and I'll have you know that Uncle pretends to be ill twice a year," Elizabeth returned heatedly. "It is only so he can send for me. He thinks . . . thinks I am too much alone," she ended softly. "Please"—her voice regained some of its strength—"release my hand. I will trouble you no further," she added, a strange chill causing her to shudder at his grip.

Something in her voice, in the tremble he felt running through her, smote the man's conscience. Raising her hand to his lips, he kissed it and quickly released his hold.

Elizabeth realized a moment later that her hand was still poised in the air where he had let go of it, and she snatched it to her lap.

"My pardon for disturbing your evening," the intruder told her softly. "Why don't you try to sleep?" He handed back the squab she had given him. "I shall be leaving you at the first inn we pass," he assured her, "and never again will our paths cross."

Her desire to ask his name was firmly squashed as Miss Jeffries accepted the pillow and forced herself to lean against it and close her eyes. The odd fluttering of her heart was adamantly commanded to end. *You shall never see this rogue again*, she told herself firmly. *Know yourself to be fortunate*.

Sleep slowly descended, dispelling all her spinsterly reproaches and allowing a dream of love and family to creep in once more.

The hint of dawn brought a grey light to the coach's interior. The cloaked man had been studying the sleeping figure for some time, his thoughts oddly disrupted. *She is not beautiful*, he concluded, *but most pleasant to gaze upon. I wonder if her eyes are dark like her hair.* He shook himself. What had happened to his sense? Had that knock on the head a week past damaged his reasoning? This was only a chance encounter with a perfectly unreasonable chit who had neither the sense to be hysterical at his intrusion nor the folly to throw herself willingly into his arms. They would never meet again. He did not even know her name. *I wonder if it is a harsh sound like Abigail, or something soothing like Letitia?* he wondered, smiling. *Certes, she is headstrong.* His eyes narrowed as he continued to study her. *Innocence . . . she has that look of innocence I had forgotten a woman could have,* he realized, and became alarmed at the trend of his thinking.

The coach slowed. They passed the outer cottages of a small village.

I must go, he thought, and quelled the urge to stay. Leaning forward, he kissed her gently and then slipped quietly out of the coach, hurrying into the shadows before anyone could see him.

Sir Henry Jeffries' comfortably rambling mansion, Ashly, sat snugly atop a hill just outside of Ashford. It was early morn when his coach, carrying his niece, halted before the large double doors of its main entry. Elizabeth Jeffries stepped down from the coach before the butler, Niles, could reach its door. "How is Uncle?" she asked.

"Improved, miss," Niles answered, his face expressionless as he recalled the late hour of his master's guests' departure last eve. "He is resting now."

"Very good," she smiled, walking towards the doors. "Please see to my portmanteaus. I believe I shall refresh myself before seeing Uncle. Will breakfast be served at nine as usual?"

"Yes, miss."

"If my uncle awakens, please tell him I had a pleasant journey. Except, of course, for the intruder. . . ." A hint of a smile came to her features.

"Would there be anything else, miss?" Niles questioned with barely concealed interest.

"No. Tell him I shall come to him as soon as I have breakfasted." She turned and walked towards the stairs.

"Miss . . ."

"Yes, Niles? What is it?"

"I believe you would like to know that Lady Waddington is to arrive later this morn," he informed her.

"Thank you, Niles," Elizabeth answered with a sigh, her already depressed spirits further dampened by the news of her aunt's imminent arrival.

The Green Room's cheerful interior did not have its usual brightening effect on Elizabeth. Laying her gloves and pelisse on the bed, she washed her hands and face. With a heavy sigh the young woman moved slowly to the oriel window overlooking the valley below. Leaning against the edge, Elizabeth gazed at the fog-shrouded village of Ashford. The buildings were visible in brief glimpses as the heavy mist slowly drifted through the streets. A ray of morning sun splashed through a break in the clouds, then was gone.

My life has become like those buildings, enveloped in doubt, she mused. *What has happened to all my certainty, to the days when peace and quiet were as-*

sured? At four and twenty there should be few additional questions to ask.

Elizabeth's thoughts drifted to the cloaked intruder, a gentle smile coming to her lips. *How tall he must be*, she thought, recalling how his head had almost touched the roof of the coach. And his form, the fine line of his leg and that broad muscular chest. . . . She sighed. *How senseless—no, how unladylike*, she amended, thinking of what her Aunt Waddie would have said to such thoughts.

While Miss Jeffries had never worried about being unladylike, she prided herself on her good sense, which seemed to be sadly lacking in this instance. What kind of sense prompted her to be saddened when, awakened by the stranger's gentle kiss, she had seen only the tail of his cloak as he slipped into the shadows. What caused this melancholy she had felt upon realizing that she would never see him again, her nameless rogue? Turning from the window, she raised her head, the line of her jaw hardening. *Enough of this, miss*, she told herself sternly. *You could not even recognize the man if you encountered him again.* Her heart begged to differ, but she quelled the instinct. A hearty breakfast was what she needed. Hunger was the cause of these nonsensical thoughts. Elizabeth marched to the door and grasped the knob, then sighed, her shoulders sagging.

Recalling the grip of his hand upon hers, she thought. *He neither robbed nor ravished me and certainly didn't frighten me.* Her features lightened, a grin spreading across them. *Mayhaps I could scandal-*

ize Aunt Waddie enough with the tale, she thought, *to have her decide to return to London immediately.* "Shameful creature," she admonished herself out loud the next instant. Chuckling, she opened the door and ambled towards the breakfast room.

Niles assisted Sir Henry into his old-fashioned frock coat. "Do you think it wise to go down, sir?" he asked.

"Confound it, Elizabeth is no child. She knows the lay of things."

"Yes, sir."

"If only Madeline did not arrive today also," Sir Henry muttered to himself, adjusting his stock. Checking his appearance one last time, he bobbed his head approvingly and made for his breakfast.

"Good morn, Elizabeth," he greeted his niece cheerfully, brushing her cheek with a kiss. Taking a plate, he chose sparingly from the dishes on the sideboard before joining her at the table.

Miss Jeffries pushed aside *The Times*, which she had been reading, and gazed sternly at her uncle.

"Just the thought of you with me for the next month worked a marvel on my health," he blustered, a soft red hue covering his face to the top of his balding pate. "You see, I am eating sparsely this morn."

"You *always* eat sparingly, Uncle," she reminded him, inspecting his lean, angular form for any hint of malady.

"Still the same young woman," he snorted, then beamed approvingly.

She burst into laughter. "You are a wonder, Uncle

Henry. I begin to see why your paternity is sometimes questioned. You differ so greatly from dear Papa and Aunt Waddie."

Choking, Sir Henry drank deeply of his tea. "Pray, my dear girl, do not go about vocalizing such indelicate thoughts. Especially not in front of Madeline. Your aunt would fly into the boughs and not be done with it for a week."

"But I have heard her say the same."

"That is different. She is a married, well, widowed lady. Now don't cast such a black look at me. I mean to abide by our truce."

"No beaux . . . no dandies . . . not even a promising solicitor?" Elizabeth questioned suspiciously, her uncle's matchmaking propensities sharply in mind.

"Well . . . Perhaps a young barrister I met last month will call while you are here. But he has been invited only because of a common interest we share," he hastened to add.

"Women?"

"Elizabeth!"

"I'm sorry, Uncle, but each time I come you throw all manner of men at me. It is so obvious—so embarrassing—to be paraded about like a shank of beef. I am happy as I am."

"You know I do not mean to—"

"Then don't. Find yourself a wife or take a mistress. Aunt Lettie has been gone five years now. You have never adjusted to being alone. . . ."

"Which is why you should agree to stay with me permanently. I told you when your father died two years past that you were welcome," Sir Henry told her earnestly.

"Even with Papa gone I must still maintain the house for Morton." Her eyes went to her plate.

"Your brother doesn't care a fiddle for that house. Hasn't cared for anything since he saw his first ship."

"And who do we have to thank for encouraging that interest? It was you who provided for his entry into the Naval Academy at Portsmouth, who arranged for his promotion on the *Zenphone*." Elizabeth's features softened upon seeing her uncle's distress. She reached across the table and placed her hand atop his. "You are not to blame for what happened. I *know* the sea is Morton's life, that it shall always be. You could not have done better by him. We both know Father had very little capital and could manage nothing. Something shall happen, you shall see. Morton may even manage to escape the French, as Sir Sydney Smith did in '98."

"This damnable war. If only Malmesbury had been successful in '96, but the French were not wishing for peace then. Their treatment of the Old Lion in '97 was proof of that. Now both governments refuse to exchange prisoners. What stupidity!" His fork clattered onto his plate.

Elizabeth's face had darkened at mention of the French. The war had made little impression upon her at its start. In the second year, however, a cousin had joined the émigrés who had landed at Quiberon Bay, and the tale of how he had been wounded, abandoned by his companions, and then died had shocked her, turning her not only against the French but against the royalists who were flocking to England for safety. Her brother's capture off Brest by the French navy intensified her feelings. She blamed her father's death on the resultant heartache and worry, and she hardened her heart further, becoming unrelenting in her prejudice, despite her uncle's entreatries to be reasonable.

"Let's have none of your nonsense about the loyalists," Sir Henry reminded her. "Madeline will probably bring a few with her. Remember Morton's last letter? How he told about the man who was giving him food and wine? What of those who smuggle his letters to the coast for us?"

"They do it only for the money it gains them. That is the sole reason. If they did not help his letters, you could not send him money—money which they take. A Frenchman would never do anything for anyone without being paid," she ended adamantly.

"Elizabeth, you are showing an absurdly ignorant streak." Her uncle shook a finger at her. "I prided myself on thinking you had better judgment than you are now showing. Just as all Englishmen are not good, all Frenchmen are not bad."

"That has not been proven to me," his niece insisted stubbornly.

He shook his head regretfully, for he regarded this unquestioning condemnation as unfortunate. His fork halted halfway to his mouth, a sudden recollection of Niles' comment coming to mind.

"What did happen on your journey?"

Colour surged to Elizabeth's cheeks. "It was nothing," she said, attacking the beef on her plate.

"Come now, you wouldn't blush so. . . . Certes you were not robbed?"

"No, Uncle. A man simply bolted into the coach as we were leaving Folkestone," she said, dismissing the incident.

"A stranger? What was his name? I'm surprised that Brown allowed it. He knows I dislike your traveling unchaperoned. I must speak with him. . . ."

"Brown knew nothing about it," Elizabeth defended the coachman. "The man simply climbed in when we slowed to round a corner. You don't know him and neither do I. He was being chased by the king's men and used your coach to escape them. I don't wish to discuss this any further," she ended, and rose. Throwing her napkin onto the table, Elizabeth strode from the room without a further word or look.

Sir Henry stared after her. Even the royalists had never elicited such a strong reaction in her. *Perhaps this man is the one I should be searching for instead of that new barrister*, he thought. *If only his name could be learned.* "I would give much to meet a man that could unsettle Elizabeth," Sir Henry mused aloud. "He must have been a most curious rogue."

Chapter III

The cloak was drawn tightly about the tall, dark man as his hired hack plodded through a field near Ashford. Finding his thoughts more melancholy than usual, he reminded himself of the success he had had in his mission and of the little Parisian wench who had entertained him so well. But when he tried to picture her, there came instead the vision of the young miss whose coach he had left but hours before. *Likely safe at her uncle's now*, he thought, grinning with the remembrance of how she had tried to take his pistol. Plenty of spirit there. He straightened with an idea. "It would be best if we got to London as quickly as possible," he told the hired beast, "but then I've seldom done what is wisest." He turned the steed towards Ashford and urged him to a gallop.

Halting before the Crown and Sword, an inn on the outskirts of town, the man lithely stepped down and drew off his cloak. After tying it behind the saddle, he strode inside and tossed a coin carelessly upon the bar.

The proprietor's pudgy, dirt-stained hand closed

over it, a toothless smile giving greeting. "Take a seat, sir. I'll fetch ye a pint o' ale." He drew a mug of rich, warm ale and carried it to the table. "Be ye travelin' ta London?" he asked, setting the mug down with a splattering jolt.

"Perhaps." The dark eyes forced the innkeeper to drop his own.

"Ye look worn," the fat man mumbled, rubbing his dirty hands on his equally filthy apron. "Thought ye might want a room."

"You have a magistrate in Ashford?" The man's gaze remained unwavering.

"Magistrates all about England," the innkeeper answered, unsettled by the light in the stranger's eye. "What need ye be havin' with a magistrate?"

"His name?" the other commanded.

The innkeeper debated his answer, then stiffened as the man leaned back in his chair, a hand coming to rest near the butt of a pistol in his waistband. "Jeffries it be, sir. Sir Henry Jeffries. I best be about me duties," he added, beginning to edge away from the table.

"Does he have a niece?"

"I've heard tell he does," the innkeeper answered slowly.

"Do you know her name?"

"Seems me heard tell o' it . . . but then his lordship be a mite above me an' we don't deal together, common like." His fat hands rubbed his double chin.

A coin appeared as if by magic in the dark man's hand. He flipped it to the innkeeper.

33

"'Lizabeth, sir. Miss 'Lizabeth Jeffries." The man beamed greedily. "There be more ye wish to be knowin'?" he asked hopefully, coming nearer.

"Bring me bread and cheese," the other commanded coldly, his face impassive.

With a regretful grimace, the innkeeper turned away.

What a fool you are, the man thought, running a hand slowly through his thick coal-black hair. *Exposing yourself needlessly to learn a chit's name, and it being Elizabeth at that.*

It was a strong proud name just like the lady. The innkeeper's return interrupted his thoughts, and he concentrated on devouring the cheese and bread. Finishing, he quaffed the last of his ale, and after placing coins on the table, he strode from the inn, swung easily into his saddle, and spurred away.

"That be a most curious sort," the innkeeper mumbled as he scraped crumbs from the table, letting them fall to the litter-covered floor. *Wonder if Sir Henry be interested in knowin' the like o' that sort are askin' after his niece?*

The thought was still on his mind a short time later when five soldiers entered the inn. After ordering ale, the sergeant asked, "Have ye seen the like o' a tall, dark man? A mean look he had and likely carryin' a pistol. He would have come by way of Folkestone."

"With hair as black as the devil's stone?" the innkeeper asked.

"Aye, an' eyes that match it."

"Who be he?"

"By name, Martin. He moves back an' forth 'tween

here and France like there 'twasn't no war. But he went too far when he threw Lord Fromby into the Channel. His lordship's set a fire to the tail on them in London, and we've ten score men sent to capture him."

"Ten score . . . all fer one man?" the other questioned skeptically.

" 'Tis the country's honour at stake ta hear his lordship," the sergeant returned, thumping his hand upon the counter.

"What did ye say this Martin did to Lord . . . ?"

"His lordship was bein' patriotic like an' gettin' information on some smugglers, so he says, when this Martin came and 'umiliated him. Pulled his fancy wig off." He winked. "His lordship be balder 'n a hen's egg, so it's told now. Then the bloke threw him over the side." The sergeant ended there, thinking it imprudent to add that his lordship had been in the company of some doubtful ladies who had preferred the assailant. Nor did he think it wise to mention that tattle in the barracks had it that Lord Fromby, for all the personal insult he had suffered, was more likely angered because the man had also made off with his ship and the cargo his lordship had arranged to be smuggled in. "Have ye seen the man?" he asked again, his ale finished.

"Aye, not two hours past. Headin' fer London he likely were."

"If ye see him again, send word to Colonel Trumbel at Dover. Lord Fromby's puttin' a large sum of guineas to the man responsible for catchin' him."

* * *

His third rented hack of the day was well lathered by the time Martin reached London. He had gone over six and thirty hours without sleep. Instead of directing his tired steed towards his own quarters, he made for a house on the edge of Mayfair which he had rented for a young lady with whom he had an amicable agreement. Discontent had lain heavily upon Martin all day and pressed him harder as he neared his destination. Even memories of Teresa's softly curved body and willing ways could not dispel this vague but stubborn dissatisfaction.

Entering the house by the back door, Martin took the main staircase two steps at a time and strode purposefully down the corridor towards the master bedchamber.

"Martin!" the powdered and painted demirep seated before the dressing table said in a strangled voice, seeing his image in her mirror.

"I did not mean to frighten you, my dear," he said, coming closer and twining a curl about his finger. "Are you not happy to see me?"

"But of course, my darling," she said in an altered tone, not quite concealing her nervousness. "Why do you look at me so strangely?" Teresa managed a gurgling laugh as she rose and turned towards him. "Is something wrong? But you tease me, that is it. You have been gone so long. What did you bring me?" An avaricious gleam came into her eye. Pausing, she deftly arched her back, raising a shoulder slightly so he could see the fullness of her breasts beneath her sheer dressing gown. She swayed towards him enticingly, a beguiling smile upon her lips. "You are happy to see me?"

she asked, twining her arms around his neck. "What did you bring me?" Her hands softly ruffled his black mane as his lips brushed hers.

Martin's hands tightened about her waist, pressing her away as he gazed at her powdered and rouged face, the eyes closed, lips awaiting him. A question appeared on his features; he hesitated. Pushing aside all doubt, he fiercely claimed her lips. Drawing back, Martin felt a faint disappointment, which he carefully concealed. Before he could speak, a sharp knock sounded on the door.

"Teresa," a plaintive male voice called.

The woman in his arms gulped as Martin lifted an eyebrow disdainfully. "I have been gone a long time," he noted as he slowly released her.

"He don't mean nothing to me, Martin, truly. I was just lonely," Teresa whined.

"I'll send a settlement, my dear," he told her as he walked to the door.

"You were gone *so* long . . ."

"You shall have no problem finding another protector, dear girl. Your ways are quite winning." *If you could but control your greed*, he thought to himself. It was a common flaw in women. "Come in," he said evenly, opening the door and greeting a startled young man. "The lady and I are finished," he noted, and walked down the corridor, his back straight, his head up, his eyes and ears closed to the epitaphs being hurled at him by his once adoring mistress.

In the street Martin mounted and prodded his beast to a trot. Achieving Piccadilly and Berkeley, he paid a beggar lad to take the horse to the nearest coaching yard, giving instructions and coin for its return to its owner. This done, he fled into the darkness, moving swiftly and silently among the alleyways. Entering a second house through the servants' entrance, he unlocked another door just inside that entry, stepped into the small closet behind it, and relocked the door. The false back of the closet was opened and the upper floor reached through a secret passageway with ease gained from long practice. At the end of the corridor Martin released the lever on the false panel and eased his tall form through the small opening into a darkened room. In the shrouding darkness he stripped to the buff, tossing his clothing back into the secret corridor. By counting his steps he safely reached the side of a large bed and pulled on the long, flowing robe which was lying on it.

Martin moved to the bedside table and lit the candle upon it, then moved about the room lighting the lamps and wall sconces. The large bedchamber thus revealed seemed at odds with the tall, muscular man. The fine oak panels covering the walls had been bleached and were etched with delicate tracings of flowers and vines which had been painted in delicate shades. Louis Quatorze furniture, with its dainty, ornate lines, contrasted sharply with the broad-shouldered and strong-featured man. Voluptuous nude maidens of sixteenth-century Venice painted by Sebastiano del Piombo adorned the two panels on either side of the fireplace. The damask drapes covering the large window on the west wall were edged in delicate French lace. An ornate, lacquered shaving stand was the only piece of obviously masculine furniture in the room, and it, too, was copiously decorated with a feminine touch.

Standing before a full-length mirror framed by rococo ormolu mounts, the tall man gazed at his reflection. The full wine-coloured gown had been cut in such a way that it diminished the broadness of his shoulders and de-emphasized his above-average height. As he gazed, a gradual transformation occurred. One shoulder was dropped slightly as he tilted his head to one side. The strong lines of his features faded; his mouth assumed a pursed look and twitched at one side. Powder and rouge were skillfully applied. Sauntering to a chair by the fire in a light, tripping step when this was done, the man pulled the bell cord before sitting.

A timid knock soon sounded upon the door, followed by a nervous, "Monseigneur le Comte, we did not know you had returned from Oatlands. Please forgive me for not coming sooner."

"It is of no import. I must bathe immediately. You know I cannot abide the filth encountered in others' homes. Lady York is a dear, but her dogs. La, one trips over them everywhere. I don't know why Brummell is such an eager guest there. My water now, at once. Come, come, we must hurry." The man in the chair by the fireplace wearily fluttered a lace kerchief in dismissal.

Mr. Leveque closed the door quietly. He had been in this establishment but a year and still found it difficult to serve his master. "How did the comte enter?"

He muttered as he hurried to order the water taken to the bedchamber. Best not to ponder it, he reprimanded himself. The Comte de Cavilon was known to be curious in his habits and to dismiss anyone who questioned anything.

"This cravat will never do," the slightly nasal tone of the comte told Leveque. "Redo it."

With an inner sigh the valet removed the offending linen and replaced it with a fresh one.

"I shall see to this one myself," Cavilon ordered with exaggerated pique, then deftly arranged it into the perfect folds of the currently popular "cascade" style. Adjusting the lace on his shirt cuffs, he examined his appearance carefully. The mauve jacket and breeches were styled in such a way as to be loose fitting in some areas and very tight fitting in others, so that he carried himself at a tilt, thus appearing much smaller than he actually was. His black mass of hair was now covered with a bag wig—elegant, if out of fashion—and held in the queue style by a massive mauve bow. A light layer of powder covered his ungentlemanly tanned features, and rouge reddened his lips. "What of my patches, Leveque? Never mind, my dear man, I shall not be seen by anyone of import this eve. Come, come, where are my kerchiefs?"

The valet brought a tray filled with lace-edged linen and silk squares.

Choosing one with a double frilled edging, the comte placed it in an inner pocket of his cutaway jacket. A second of the same size worked in silver thread was placed behind his watch in the pocket of his smallclothes. A third, ruched in three-inch lace, was tucked into his cuff band. "And my boxes, must have my boxes, Leveque," he prattled.

A second tray of an assortment of elegant and costly snuffboxes and pill cases was brought forward. These varied from delicate enamels to heavier ceramics to bejeweled and gold-leafed marvels. Choosing two, Cavilon placed them in the tooled-leather bag upon the commode, then placed the strap of the pack over his shoulder. "Order my coach, my closed coach, of course. I do believe I am ready." He breathed a delicate sigh of relief as he paused before his looking glass once more.

The stilted pose was eased several seconds after the door closed behind the valet. For a long moment Cavilon glared with distaste at the powdered face gazing back at him, then resumed all the affectations that achieved the startling alteration in his looks. There was no trace of the man Martin to be seen when he left the room. His transformation was complete.

Chapter IV

Arriving outside No. 41 Grosvenor Square, the Comte de Cavilon stepped from his closed coach with exaggerated steps and minced to the door. His footman rushed to lift the door knocker for him.

"The Comte de Cavilon to see the Earl of Tretain," the footman told the butler when the door opened.

"Lord Tretain will be most pleased to see you, my lord," the butler told the comte, ignoring the footman and taking his lordship's hat and gloves. "My lord is in the library."

"I shall go on my own, Homer." Cavilon waved his kerchief from his cuff and headed towards the library with the light, tilted pose by which all recognized him.

"Louis!" Lord Adrian Tretain's face lit up with pleasure at the sight of his friend. "From the gossip floating about London I was fearful for you. When did you return? Come sit." The earl pulled a bell cord as Cavilon swayed into position on the sofa at one side of the fireplace. "See we are not disturbed," he instructed Homer, and went to his seat as the butler closed the doors. After carefully scrutinizing his friend, he noted,

"You look exhausted. Would you care for some brandy or port?"

"And after I was so very careful with my toilet." Cavilon sighed and daubed at the corner of his eye.

"The trip was that difficult?" Tretain shook his head unsympathetically.

"Brandy," Cavilon told him, slowly relaxing but not entirely dropping his pose. "Mayhaps it is time I tried in earnest to become a four-bottle man," he said lightly.

Tretain peered sharply at the comte as he filled the glasses. "There is word about London that Lord Fromby has offered a reward for a smuggler by the name of Martin. He even implies the man is a traitor. The Admiralty has been forced to send a special assignment of men to find him."

"Then Martin had better beware." Cavilon arched a brow.

"There was trouble?" Tretain handed the glass to the comte.

Cavilon took a sip, then drank more than half the glass. "There was an unusually large group of excise men on the shore to bid me welcome," he said cryptically.

"I thought a Frenchman was taught from birth to savour his *liqueur*," Tretain commented, refilling the other's glass before sitting across from him.

"Pass these on as usual." Cavilon drew a sheaf of papers from the purse beneath his arm. "The Admiralty will find them interesting as well as useful."

"How did you escape the excise men?" the earl asked, accepting the papers.

"It was not very difficult, but it was odd to find them placed as they were. They not only had the area where we landed surrounded but also knew the direction of the farm."

"Did they take anyone?"

"I believe all escaped when I drove the officers' mounts through the fray on the beach. I am grateful the king's men can afford such excellent beasts," he said, and smiled. "Else I would not have evaded those waiting me at the farm."

"Awaiting you? This is serious. Just what did you do to Fromby?" Tretain asked, leaning back in his chair.

"I simply gave the pompous ass a lesson in deportment, although he did not take too well to the water. You had better see what can be done to control his enthusiasm for finding Martin. I don't mind playing games with Bonaparte's men, but I would prefer not to be regarded as a pheasant in season here," Cavilon told him wryly.

"It is time you took a rest. You have dared too much for too long."

"I believe you are correct," the comte agreed, to the other's surprise. "It is no longer a distraction."

"What troubles you, *bon ami*?" Tretain asked softly.

Cavilon stared at him for a long moment, then his eyes moved to the fire burning brightly in the grate. "Perhaps I am like a fire that has burned too brilliantly for too long. The flame to avenge my family, lost in the bloodbath of the revolution, the loss of my home, my lands . . . my country—it was all-consuming for a time. The danger, the risk, was but fuel for the flame. Each challenge, once conquered, drew me to the next. It became a game."

"I recall that feeling," Tretain reminisced. "The excitement of the chase, of overcoming all odds. Before I met my Juliane I was much the same as you. Even now there are odd moments when I wonder if I should have given it up so completely. But they are very few." His eyes rose to the portrait of his wife above the fireplace.

The comte's eyes followed his friend's. "Yours was a most unusual courtship, as I recall it." He smiled. "You have had no regrets?"

"None," the earl assured him. "You must call when you can see the children."

"I never thought to hear such words from you," Cavilon teased. "Do you remember those four ladies we entertained in Trier for a week? What about Versailles, when you were forced to flee in only your nightshirt?"

"At least that was better than the time those *chevaliers* caught you in the bath with Lady Breaux," Tretain countered, and both men broke into laughter.

The earl noticed that Cavilon's gaiety quickly faded, replaced by a restlessness he had seen growing in the other man for some time. "There are compensations that make such recollections small," he offered gently. "Children . . ."

"Is Juliane breeding again?"

A proud smile came to Tretain's face. "Yes, our sixth."

"You mean fourth, do you not?" the comte corrected.

"Well, yes, but André and Leora seem like our own. Leora was little more than a babe when we wed."

"How do your young nephew and niece fare?"

"André is at Christ Church Oxford and doing very well. He is anxious for the day when he can join the war. But that is natural, having lost his mother to the French as he did. Leora is all of seven now and still in the nursery with our own three."

"Perhaps you shall have a second son this time," Cavilon mused.

"It matters not, although Mother would cringe if she heard me say that."

The comte chuckled at the thought of the Dowager Countess of Tretain. "How is she?" he asked.

"Very well for her age. She enjoys having the children about."

"How *domestique* you have become with all this talk of children," Cavilon said more sharply than he had intended. He finished his brandy, rose, and refilled his glass.

"What troubles you?" Tretain questioned a second time, puzzled by his friend's unusual lack of composure. Something had occurred to shake the iron calm the comte had always maintained.

Cavilon swung about abruptly. "When you met Juliane, were you certain . . . I mean did you feel . . ." His voice faded as he groped for words.

"You don't mean to wed at last?" Tretain exclaimed, then lifted an eyebrow. "Certes not that lightskirt you keep at—"

"No," the comte answered curtly. "That was ended this eve," he continued in a milder tone. "I fear I was gone too long. Those situations are not long-lived in any event," he concluded, dismissing the subject.

"Then who?" Tretain asked, puzzled.

"No one," Cavilon returned. "The voyage across the Channel was rough, and I have not slept for two days. I begin to ramble. The joy has gone out of the game. I have tired of it. Of this, too." He waved the lace kerchief.

"The pretense serves you—and all England—well," the earl told him, admiration for the other filling his words.

"It may soon be time for it to end," Cavilon mused. "I believe I shall look about England for an estate, something which would fill my time."

"There are lands for sale near Trees," Tretain began, his eyes brightening at mention of his country seat.

"No, I was thinking more of the eastern counties. I am, after all, more familiar with them." He sipped his brandy. "Yes, perhaps near Ashford." Rising, he held out his hand. "Give my best to Juliane. I take it all is well with her?"

"Yes, it is early days yet. Her confinement will be late in the summer. Why don't you come to supper tomorrow? She will be angry at having missed you."

"I shall send word later. I may leave in the morn."

"What, without seeing me?" a light voice asked. The two men turned to the library's doors. "Homer told me you had come," Lady Juliane added, approaching them. "You did not mean to leave without seeing me?" she questioned accusingly, a smile belying her tone.

"It is always a delight to see you." Cavilon bowed

with a flourish, his kerchief trailing on the carpet. "You are the only sensible woman I have ever found in England. How sad you are already wed." He sighed dramatically.

"Stop that nonsense," Lady Juliane laughed. The earl stepped to her side and put his arm about her waist.

An odd look came to Cavilon as he gazed upon the happy couple. "I fear I must bid you adieu." He took Lady Juliane's hand and kissed it lightly. "You are most fortunate," he told Tretain gruffly, and strode past them before either could speak.

"What has come over Louis?" Juliane asked.

"I think he may have met a second 'sensible' woman and does not quite know what to do," Tretain said, putting his arms about his wife.

"Did he say something . . . mention a name?" She questioned eagerly.

"No, my dear, to both questions. I think he almost did, but Louis has never been very open about such matters."

"He has been open enough about the courtesans he keeps."

"But they meant nothing to him," the earl said gently.

"Has there ever been anyone?"

"Many years past there was the daughter of a French duc. Rosamon was her name, but he has not spoken of her since the days of gore in Paris. I do not even know if she perished there. His look was so black when I began to speak of her one day that I have not brought it up since.

"Now, my love," he cupped her chin gently, "why don't we leave Louis and his love, if there be one, to solve their own problems?"

"Of course, my lord," she answered, mentally adding a "for now" before losing the thought as the earl's lips claimed hers.

The supper table in Sir Henry Jeffries' dining room seated twelve guests this night, and while his dinner parties were known for their cuisine, intelligent conversation and good humour, only the food was saving this evening from total failure.

Sir Henry had never seen his niece in such fitful temper. On the ordinary she was pleasant if not biddable, and witty rather than spiteful. Such were her words this eve, when she did speak, that Mr. Wayne, the young barrister at her right, had long since concerned himself with his food only. Even Lady Madeline had grown silent beneath Elizabeth's sharp replies and the five French émigrés who had come with her were hoping for an early end to the evening. Only Suzanne Chatworth, daughter of a business acquaintance, and his wife, remained unperturbed and chatted gaily with Sir Henry and Monsieur Manc.

"Let us excuse ourselves, ladies," Lady Waddington signaled an end to the meal. "We shall leave you gentlemen to your port." A meaningful glance was cast at Elizabeth, who rose dutifully and led the way to the large salon where a fire was burning brightly and tea awaited.

Mrs. Chatworth and her daughter sat on the sofa while Lady Waddington maneuvered the French ladies, Madame Moné and Madame Turren, to chairs close by the fire before seating herself. "Come, Elizabeth, sit down," Aunt Waddie commanded, pointing to a chair near the Chatworths.

"I am quite capable of doing that on my own," Miss Jeffries snapped, instantly regretting the outburst as she had many of her actions and words this eve.

"Perhaps you should sit close to the fire," Suzanne offered innocently. "A chill can bring on the crotchets in one your age," she teased.

"Are you feeling quite well, Miss Jeffries?" Mrs. Chatworth's words followed sharply on her daughter's. "I could not help but notice that you did not seem yourself this eve," she added, trying to ease the tension.

"Elizabeth has not yet recovered from the severe fright she was dealt just two eves past," Lady Waddington entered the conversation determinedly. "And quite understandable in a young woman of her sensibilities. Can you imagine how it would be to have a ruffian force his way into your coach?" She posed the question dramatically.

Gasps came from the four women; their eyes flew to Elizabeth.

"Why, he forced his way in and forced Elizabeth to help him escape the king's men," Lady Waddington explained with the verve of a practiced gossip. "You can imagine how unsettling it was. It is quite natural she has not yet recovered."

"You know I was *not* unsettled by the incident in the least," Elizabeth noted acidly. "And he did not use force. . . ."

"As I was saying," Aunt Waddie spoke loudly, "Elizabeth is not feeling well."

" 'Pon my soul, Elizabeth," exclaimed Suzanne. "If it had happened to me, I would have fainted, I am certain, or at least gone into high hysterics. But you always did have more . . . Well, you know how delicate I am." She sighed.

Hoping to ease matters, Mrs. Chatworth asked, "Have you heard from your brother recently, Miss Jeffries?"

"Our last letter arrived two months past. We are hopeful of hearing again soon, but it is very difficult to get letters through. It takes many bribes." Her eyes went to the two French ladies.

"Your brother is a *captif* of Bonaparte, *n'est-ce pas?*" Madame Moné asked, meeting the glance unflinchingly.

"Yes, his ship was taken off Brest more than four and twenty months past," Elizabeth answered coldly.

"We do hope he has not fared too badly," Madame Turren offered kindly.

"Do you?"

"Elizabeth," Lady Waddington spoke sharply. "Perhaps our guests would like some music. Why don't you and Miss Chatworth play one of your delightful duets on the pianoforte?"

"Come, let's do." Suzanne rose eagerly. "I know it will raise your spirits," she whispered, taking Elizabeth's hand.

Miss Jeffries rose but was very doubtful of the truth of those words. The entire evening had become a series of sharp retorts to others and reprimands to herself. "Let us play 'Triste Carmine,'" she suggested as they sat at the piano.

"But that is such a sad melody," Suzanne objected, finally acceding with a sigh.

The melancholy air filled the room as the young ladies applied themselves to it with skill. Aunt Waddie looked at her niece searchingly. Her behaviour was distinctly at odds with her usual charming demeanour.

Elizabeth had never played better, for her heart lent a new depth to the music, expressing a deep, frustrating sorrow she could not understand.

Chapter V

"I am so glad you decided to remain in London for a time," Lady Juliane told the Comte de Cavilon a few days after his evening call, as they seated themselves on a bench in St. James's Park. The afternoon sunshine of early April was warming the spirits of many, including her ladyship's two young daughters. "You mustn't pull your sister's hair," she called out sternly to the younger, who had a determined hold on her sister Michelle's locks. "I fear Anne Marie is going to be a great deal like me," she sighed, watching long enough to ensure compliance.

"And what is to be feared in that?" Cavilon smiled. "She is a beautiful child."

"But more towards the hoyden than the lady," Lady Juliane answered pensively. "I have no fears for Michelle's successful entry into society when the time comes. She is already conscious of her looks and only six years of age. Why, I must have been six and twenty before I . . ." She laughed at herself, shaking her head. "Now Anne Marie, even though only four, is concerned solely with defending her rights."

"For my part a woman who is not overly concerned

with her looks would be a vast relief." The comte's eyes strayed to the children. "If Anne Marie had a score more years, mayhaps I could be persuaded to . . ."

"Fah, you are the eternal bachelor, Louis," Lady Juliane teased. "What woman would dare vie with your magnificence?" she asked, waving a hand at his elaborate toilet. "Although I do think you should desist in wearing those powdered perukes. They are just not the style."

Cavilon sighed, sagging into a crestfallen pose.

"Why, Louis, I had no idea they meant so much to you. I did not mean . . ."

He looked at her with woebegone eyes. "Even you, Juliane? My only hope for English womanhood, concerned with style? La, women are all the same."

"You are teasing again, Louis. When will you become serious? I—"

"Why, Lady Tretain, how nice to see you." The large, turbaned bulk of Lady Reed blocked the sunshine. "Are those two adorable cherubs your daughters?" she gushed as she halted before her ladyship. "What a charming picture they present. Much like my own dear Barbara before she came from the schoolroom." The proud mama maneuvered her daughter into Cavilon's view.

Taking the lady's words with an inner sigh, for Anne Marie was at the moment tackling Michelle, Lady Juliane nodded a greeting. "How nice to see you," she said, hoping this was to be a brief encounter, for there was much she wanted to ask the comte.

"I don't believe you have ever met my Barbara." Lady Reed prodded the girl forward.

Miss Reed, just come from the schoolroom this season, blushed fiercely but curtsied, her eyes fast upon the grass.

"Of course you know the Comte de Cavilon, Lady Reed," Lady Juliane said when the matron's look told her she would remain until introduced. She barely suppressed a fit of giggles as Cavilon wriggled his nose and cocked his head in acknowledging the woman.

"La, what a pleasure." He waved his kerchief wearily.

"A most decided pleasure," Lady Reed beamed. "I saw you at Mr. Seibring's on Wednesday last. Perhaps your lordship would consent to grace our soirée on Thursday next?" she rushed to invite him. "I shall send a card at once," she added before he could refuse. The large woman then nudged her daughter once more.

"So . . . so pleased to make your . . . acquaintance, my lord," the young Miss Reed stammered, undone by his lordship's elegance and unnerving manner.

"We must be going." The lady fluttered a hand in farewell and marched proudly away, her purpose accomplished.

"Another conquest," Lady Juliane teased when the pair were out of hearing.

"It never ceases to amaze me," Cavilon noted dryly, raising his lace to his nose and delicately sniffing, "that no matter how odd my dress or curious my habits, the determined English mama is ever able to find credit for them. They are quite willing, nay, eager to foist their daughters into my hands."

"Your dress odd?" The Countess Tretain arched an eyebrow, a finger going to her cheek. When this drew no response, she continued more seriously. "Not everyone is eager to know you only because of your pounds sterling."

"But the rumours of my wealth procure immediate acceptance for me. Name a woman other than yourself who would fawn over me if I were poor, or who would not hurry to offer me her charms if chance of wedlock were held before her."

The bitterness in his voice shocked Lady Juliane. "There is Lady Wolhampton," she offered meekly.

"She is five and ninety." Cavilon broke into a grin and shook his head.

"You did not give any limitations," Lady Juliane smiled in relief. "But let us be serious. You . . . you are becoming too cynical, Louis," she noted sadly. "Oh, I do not deny you are correct up to a point, but there are women who hold honour more valuable than wealth. What reaction can you expect, though, the way you carry on?" she challenged. "The young ladies of the *beau monde* are raised spoiled beyond belief and taught from the cradle that they are the center of importance in the world. You challenge them by believing that exactly the same is true for you."

"Ahh, la, a true scold. It has been years since . . ." An odd look came to his eyes. For a second he saw not Lady Juliane but Elizabeth Jeffries before him.

"Louis? Louis, are you well?" Lady Tretain asked, laying a hand upon his arm.

The comte shook himself. "When have you known me to have but the best of health?" He forced a smile.

"Have you lost your funds?" Juliane asked, a sudden answer for Cavilon's recent strange behaviour occurring to her.

"No, my dear countess," he laughed, patting her hand. "The four percents are as certain as ever. Do not concern yourself. I fear I have been neglectful and bothersome this afternoon."

"Of course not. I was delighted when you called and asked to take us out. Oh, dear." She rose and rushed forward, scooping Anne Marie from atop a lad slightly larger than herself.

An irate nanny ran forward at the same time and picked up the crying lad. Tossing a quelling look at Lady Juliane, whom she thought to be an overdressed member of her own profession, she carried the boy off.

"He called me a name, Mama," Anne Marie protested, wriggling in her mother's arms.

Cavilon came up to them at his usual tilt. "Lady Tretain," he bowed exaggeratedly, waving his kerchief wildly, which distracted the little girl as he had intended, causing her to chortle. "I would be delighted to defend your honour," the comte told her with a kiss to her hand.

"Would you, Uncle Louis?" she asked excitedly. Then a question entered her eyes.

"You doubt me?" Cavilon tweaked her cheek.

"But if you did, you might muss your pretty clothes, and Michelle says you would never do that," Anne Marie told him ruefully.

"Your first lesson, *ma petite*," Cavilon took her from her mother, "is to learn to never believe all you hear about a person, nor believe just what he wishes you to see about him," he told her as he smoothed her gown over her petticoats.

"That is true for women as well as for men," Lady Juliane noted pointedly. "Come, young ladies." She took hold of Michelle's hand. "It is time we returned home."

"Oh, must we?" Anne Marie disclaimed.

"Think of your little brother. He must be lonely," she was told.

"What if I were to let you ride beside my driver?" Cavilon asked, putting her down.

"Would you?"

"People will stare at you. It would be most improper," Michelle told her primly. "Ask Mama."

Lady Juliane threw a hint of a frown at her eldest. "You may . . . if Uncle Louis rides with you. I would not like to chance the child falling," she explained in answer to his look.

"Then we shall do it. It is time I gave the town a new *on dit*. Come, let us go. I see my coach." The comte led Anne Marie forward, his heart melting beneath her grateful smile.

Handing Lady Juliane and Michelle into the coach, Cavilon ordered his driver down. "You will be so good as to ride with the footman," he told the man as he climbed onto the box. "Please hand Lady Tretain to me." Taking the little girl, he made certain she was securely seated before picking up the reins. After a nod at the footman at the team's head to release them, he flicked the reins and eased them out into the busy street.

"What was it the young man called you?" Cavilon asked, his curiosity pricked by the violence of the little girl's reaction.

"He said I was a lady," Anne Marie answered with an insulted grimace. "I told him I would rather be a hoyden, and he laughed. That's when I hit him."

"And what is a hoyden?" he asked, wondering if this little one was more knowledgeable than he supposed.

"I . . . I don't know," she answered honestly. "But Papa says he loves Mama because she is still more a hoyden than a lady."

Cavilon laughed gently. "May you never change, Anne Marie," he told her with a smile.

"Could we gallop, Uncle Louis?"

"For you, *ma belle petite*, anything."

Those who knew the comte gaped in surprise at the sight of him atop the box with the joyous little girl beside him. It was widely known that Cavilon disliked the London air and was seldom, if ever, seen in anything but his closed coach. Even more startling was that he would permit a child near him and that she was being allowed to crush the tail of his velvet coat, clinging to it as they bowled down the street.

"Here you are Elizabeth," Lady Waddington clucked, pouncing into the sewing room. "I have been trying to find you since breakfast. My lord, what are you doing?" She gazed in horror as her niece rent a wide strip of material from a linen bedsheet. It was evident from the material surrounding the young woman that several sheets had already met a similar fate.

"Wrappings . . . bandages for the wounded," Elizabeth answered, vigourously tearing another strip from the bed linen.

"Quite commendable, my dear, but what has Henry to say to this? It would not do if our guests were forced to sleep on bare mattresses."

"The émigrés should be happy to have anything to sleep on. Besides, these sheets have seen many years of service and shall not be missed. I am certain Uncle Henry would approve."

Deciding to ignore her niece's first words, her aunt attacked her last. "Elizabeth, when are you going to learn that you must always question a man before you do *anything*, even *if* you are not interested in his answer. It is the first principal of being a good wife." Lady Waddington shook her head despairingly.

"But I have no need to concern myself with such a rule," Miss Jeffries quipped, winding into a neat roll the last strip she had torn. "I have been delivered once more. Mr. Wayne took his leave this morn after breakfast."

"You should be ashamed of your treatment of that young man," her aunt scolded, taking a seat and picking up a strip, rolling it as she saw Elizabeth was doing.

"Is it my fault he was so easily cowed? I do wish

you and Uncle would find men of at least minor spirit if you must throw them in my path."

Lady Waddington eyed her skeptically. No one had ever cowed Elizabeth, nor were they ever likely to, she thought. *It is all George's fault, educating her as if she were a lad, allowing her to run the house at such an early age when her mother passed away.* Why, she had been only ten at the time.

"Why were you looking for me, Aunt?" Elizabeth's words broke into Lady Waddington's reverie.

"Oh, Madam Turren wishes to go into Ashford, and I was wondering if you could go with her. Her English is fair, but she forgets it all if she becomes flustered," Aunt Waddie continued, diligently rolling the strips.

"Why have you never bothered to learn French? Never mind." Elizabeth waved aside the usual lengthy reply she recalled this question always produced. "I suppose I could. She is such a shy creature," she answered, frowning.

"Thank you, my dear. I do appreciate the improvement in your manners this week past, but you do seem quite unusually ill-humoured. What has put you out of sorts? Are you concerned for Morton? Henry assures me all is as well for him as can be under the circumstances."

"I know, Aunt. It is not Morton. I suppose this spring weather has made me restless," Elizabeth said, bending over her work, unwilling to reveal to anyone the vivid dreams that had kept her in a state of inner turmoil ever since her encounter with the rogue.

"I have just the answer for that, my dear," Lady

Waddington told her, girding herself for the fray. "I have spoken to Henry, and we have decided you should go to London. With Henry's influence and my connections, I can assure you a stimulating time," she rushed on. "You have not been there for two years and—"

"I believe that is an excellent suggestion," Elizabeth interrupted her aunt's persuasions. "When shall we go?"

"Wh . . . when? You mean . . . you mean you consent?" Lady Waddington dropped her rolled bandage, which careened across the room till it was spent.

"It may be just the diversion I need," the young woman answered adamantly. *Where else to forget one man*, she thought, proud of her returning common sense, *than to go to a place where men abound?*

Chapter VI

"Tretain, I had not thought to encounter you here." The Comte de Cavilon minced forward through the crowd of men with a flutter of his kerchief. "What brings you to Tattersall's this fine day?"

"I must find a pony for Michelle and perhaps one for Anne Marie, if she can remain out of trouble long enough to warrant it. But enough of that. What brings you here?" the earl asked, watching the comte daub daintily at his forehead.

"I must have had to walk a complete furlong," Cavilon's voice rose in register and volume as a gentleman known to both sauntered by. "You *know* how I detest exercise of any sort."

The two began walking towards the ring, where a pair of blacks were being shown.

"Your report was very valuable," Tretain whispered in an aside. "I thought you were going to the eastern counties to purchase land," he continued in a normal tone, hard-pressed to remain serious as Cavilon dipped a shoulder with each step as he sashayed forward.

"I decided that would be . . . rash." The comte arched an eyebrow, halting beside a gentleman.

"Land is so mundane." He fluttered his kerchief in the man's face. "Isn't it, Fromby?"

"Put that damned woman's thing away, Cavilon," Lord Fromby spat. "Three hundred pounds," he called to the auctioneer.

The comte surveyed the pair, then sniffed delicately into his kerchief. "The outer one has a spavined front foreleg, Fromby. Best beware." He drew out the last words in a nasal drawl.

"Haven't you a petticoat that needs rinsing?" Fromby snorted disdainfully.

"No, but I hear you favour a salt bath for your delicate skin. A shame you couldn't convince your 'petticoats' it was worthwhile," Cavilon twittered.

Fromby's heavy, jowled cheeks flamed red as he rose to the bait. His hands flashed out and grabbed hold of the comte's jacket lapels.

"La, my lord. Leveque will be most distressed." Cavilon hung limp in the man's hold.

"Who the bloody hell is Leveque?"

"My valet. He will have to press this jacket. You are rumpling it dreadfully."

"Sold!" the auctioneer's voice boomed, jerking Fromby's head towards the ring.

"Wait," he protested, dropping his hold as he turned.

"The sale is final."

"You really should thank me." Cavilon minced the words, smoothing his wrinkled lapels. "I have saved you days, absolutely days, of worry over that foreleg. It was spavined . . . ask Tretain here." He waved his kerchief beneath the angry man's nose.

"If you were half a man, I'd press your jacket with you in it," Fromby spat, and stormed away.

"Pressing is exactly what he is suited for," Cavilon said dryly.

"Don't you fear you shall try him too far one day?" Tretain questioned as the next animal was brought in. "He may one day fail to be distracted."

"Then I shall be forced to flail him with my lace."

"He has friends in powerful positions . . ."

"What do you think of that mare, Adrian?" Cavilon's attention had shifted to the ring. "Good breeding there."

"For a lady's mount. A lovely chestnut," Tretain gave his assessment.

The bidding was opened and was quite lively for several minutes.

"Hamilton seems set upon having her," the earl noted. "I hear he has been seen oft with Harriet Wilson of late. Perhaps he means to try for her."

"Sir, oh sir." Vavilon waved his kerchief at the auctioneer. "I do believe I would rather like to make a bid."

A murmur of laughter echoed mutely through the crowd.

The auctioneer glanced about. Seeing who spoke, he doffed his hat, bowing. "My lord would like to make a bid," he announced to the men watching the proceedings. "My lord, do ye think ye could be makin' it now?" he questioned with light sarcasm.

"La, *oui*. Would six hundred pounds be sufficient?"

A heavier murmur ran through the men.

"What are you bidding on the mare for?" Tretain began. "Six hundred pounds? Cavilon, have you—"

"Make that eight hundred. My card, monsieur. Have the mare delivered this afternoon," The comte sent a boy into the ring with it. "Come, Tretain, you may take me to White's. 'Pon my soul, my good man, you can't stand about gaping." He took the earl's arm and led him away.

"You may spend your money as you wish, Louis, but eight hundred pounds for a mare? Are you thinking of taking that lightskirt back?" Tretain questioned as they rode in his coach towards White's.

"I am, and for some time to come, going to remain unattached," Cavilon assured him. "I find women a bore at present. No, I may reconsider the possibility of purchasing an estate and, of course, shall need mounts for my guests," he said smoothly.

The earl rolled his eyes and crossed his arms. "I find it difficult to believe you have survived six and thirty years in this world, Louis, mouthing such fustian as that."

"It is because I never become agitated. Calm, Adrian, one must remain calm." Before he could continue, the coach came to an abrupt halt.

"Now what?" Tretain questioned, opening the door to look out. "There has been some sort of accident just ahead of us. Looks like some young dandy didn't keep his high-perch phaeton in control. The wheels may be locked with another coach's. Let's see if we can help get them separated."

"Soil my gloves? Never." Cavilon arched an eyebrow. "But I will come and observe."

The earl shook his head as he stepped into the street. Cavilon followed, coming from the coach with exaggerated care. By the time he reached the scene of the mishap, Tretain was attempting to cool the argument about who was at fault.

"Young man, come here," an older lady called from the coach as the comte halted near it. "Sir," she repeated when he pointedly ignored her. "I say, Elizabeth, he does look French in all that lace. Could you not call him here?"

The name pricked Cavilon's ears.

"Really, Aunt Waddie, why don't we remain inside?" a voice he recognized protested.

"Madam were you wishing *mon attention*?" Cavilon turned to face the coach.

"Would you be so good as to help us down, sir? I do dislike all this jolting about."

"*Oui*, madame." The comte bowed prettily. Wiping the coach handle first, he opened the door. "You," he motioned to a beggar boy hovering nearby, "put the steps down."

"Aye, sir." The lad ran forward after catching the coin tossed his way.

"Now, Elizabeth, don't leave those boxes and tins. They will be tossed all about," Lady Waddington instructed as she took Cavilon's upraised hand.

His face remained impassive when she leaned heavily on it, coming from the coach with deliberate, ponderous movements. "How good of you, sir. I am Lady Madeline, the Marchioness Waddington," she told him as she released his hand from her tight grip.

The comte shook his fingers delicately. "*Mon plasir*,

my lady. I am the Comte de Cavilon." He made an elaborate flourish and in so doing struck the boxes and tins in Miss Jeffries' arms as she edged to the second step. The unexpected blow, combining with a sudden lurch of the coach as they attempted to back the teams in order to separate them, jostled Elizabeth. She lost her balance and began juggling her burdens in a futile effort to save them and herself from falling.

Cavilon swung about and made a desperate lunge but succeeded only in ending up beneath Miss Jeffries as she fell. A shower of peruke dusting powder from one of the boxes settled upon them in a billowing cloud.

The crowd which had gathered about the accident began coughing and waving frantically to clear the air. Miss Jeffries coughed and spluttered as the powder settled. Her eyes were flashing angrily when they met Cavilon's, half hidden by his drooping eyelids.

"La, 'pon my soul, what a good blend of powder," he quipped. "What a shame it had to ruin my jacket. Oh, my." He drew his breath in sharply.

"Are you injured, sir?" Elizabeth asked, her anger changing to concern at his expression.

"I do believe . . . Oh, my, yes, my lace is torn." The comte raised his rent kerchief for her inspection.

Disbelief filled Miss Jeffries as she stared at it. "You are concerned for that?" She grabbed it from his hand and dashed it to the ground. "Just what were you doing, pawing about in the air like that?" she demanded.

"My dear, the Comte de Cavilon does *not* paw.

Have you never seen a proper flourish? You were at fault in not allowing me to assist you," he corrected her.

"I . . . You . . . I never." She tossed her head, completely mindless that they were still sitting in the middle of the street.

"Elizabeth. Elizabeth, come," Lady Waddington urged anxiously, uncomfortably aware of the crowd gaping at the ludicrous sight of the powder-covered pair. "You must rise." She held out her hand.

"Lady Waddington is quite correct, you know," Cavilon noted, pulling a second kerchief from the pocket in his half coat. "I do believe you are putting a dreadful crease in my breeches."

"Why, you overdressed, pompous . . ." Miss Jeffries struggled to rise.

Lord Tretain appeared and helped her. "Are you quite all right, miss?" he asked. "Let me assist you." He tried to take the packages she still held.

"I am perfectly capable of taking care of myself. That," she said vehemently, nodding at the comte, "requires your aid."

The earl swallowed his grin and held out his hand to the comte. Pulling him up, he surveyed his friend with stoic reserve.

"Can our coach be freed?" Lady Waddington asked, wishing to end this episode as quickly as possible, or at least before Elizabeth could vent her ire.

Tretain issued orders which soon accomplished her wish.

"You should never hold your jaw so rigid," Cavilon

spoke casually to Miss Jeffries as he flicked at the dust upon his sleeve. "It will bring severe lines to your features," he continued in French, "but then a lady of your age has accepted such a fate." The comte motioned to the spinster's cap upon her now powdered locks.

"Apparently no one has pointed out to you that your manners are atrocious, my lord," she returned with tightly bridled anger.

"Oh, look, Elizabeth. They have separated the wheels. We can go. Come, now." Lady Waddington took hold her niece's arm.

"I am not finished, Aunt," the other returned acidly.

"That is what I feared," Aunt Waddie mumbled to herself. She cast a worried glance at the powder-covered gentleman who was standing at such an odd tilt, totally unperturbed by the appearance he presented or the threat of Elizabeth's tone. "I am sorry," she told him, tugging at her niece's arm. "Come, Elizabeth," she hardened her voice, exasperation grating in it. "You are creating a scene."

"I . . . I," Miss Jeffries stammered, shaking free of the hold. "Look at my gown, Aunt." She gave her skirts a shake, sending a cloud of powder into the air. "He did this to me and have we received one word of apology?"

"There is no need for that, miss. I understand . . . the excitement of the accident," Cavilon graciously excused her.

"You . . . You impossible . . . Ohh!" Her eyes fell upon the box which had held the dusting mixture. Picking it up, she flung what remained in it into Cavi-

70

lon's face and stalked to the coach. Elizabeth allowed Tretain to hand her in and settled herself while her aunt scrambled in and ordered the coachman onward, flinging a "thank you" from the window as they were carried away.

The people began to slowly drift away. Many a laugh and joking merriment was enjoyed over the gentleman's treatment at the hands of the angry lady.

A smile wreathing his face, the earl sauntered to where Cavilon's crumpled hat lay. After attempting to straighten it, he handed it to his friend, observing dryly, "I don't believe you said the right thing this time."

The comte accepted the hat disdainfully, ordering the beggar lad, still hovering nearby, to collect the boxes the ladies had failed to retrieve. He took them from the boy and gave him a second coin, then joined Tretain, who was awaiting him beside his coach.

"I shall give orders for the packages to be returned after we take you to your apartments. Somehow I feel White's isn't ready for your new white style," the earl managed, entering the coach after Cavilon. He broke into laughter as he dropped into his seat. "You should have seen the sight the two of you presented . . ." he began. "That young woman is a . . ." Tretain bit back his words at sight of the glint in the other's eye. "At least," he offered more soberly, "you needn't see that particular young lady again. Lady Waddington has been a stay-at-home since her husband's death. I didn't realize she had a daughter, though."

"Niece," Cavilon corrected, then brushed at his

sleeve. "Do you really think it was something I said?" he asked, cocking his head, then burst into laughter.

Tretain, joining him, only later recalled that it was the first time in months he had seen his friend truly pleased. Drawing a breath, he teased, "I do think the powder is on rather a bit thick, even for you."

Cavilon grinned wryly. "Miss Jeffries does have an interesting way of making a point, *n'est-ce pas?*"

Chapter VII

"Good lord, Madeline, Elizabeth! What happened to you?" Sir Henry Jeffries exclaimed when his sister and niece returned to Lady Waddington's home on Mount Street, where they were staying.

"There was an accident with the coach," Lady Madeline began.

"The coach? My dears, come, sit down. Bently, fetch some brandy." Sir Henry sprang forward to assist them. "How pale you look. Why, what is that all over your gowns?" He pulled his spectacles from his pocket and gave the two a closer inspection.

"We were not harmed, Uncle Henry," Elizabeth tried to calm him. "But your peruke powder did not fare as well."

"Is that what it is?" Sir Henry brushed a hand across her cheek. "Why, yes. It does nothing for your looks, my dear," he noted with a sudden twinkle in his eye.

"It did even less for the Frenchman," she said and burst into laughter, the last glimmer of her unreasonable anger suddenly gone. "You should have seen him, Uncle. Sitting there in the street in his silk breeches and that heavy brocade coat, lace at his wrists and throat. He even had powder on his face, and his lips were rouged." She surprised even herself with these details, having thought she had noticed little of the man but his foul manners. "With that peruke on his head he looked like someone belonging in London five and twenty years ago," she concluded, drawing off her gloves. "No offense meant," came more contritely when she saw her uncle's grimace, his peruke covering his balding pate. "When we left him, he had been given a free dusting. And"—Elizabth attempted to become more sober—"as poor as all the Frenchmen abounding in this country are, that should have pleased him."

"Elizabeth," Lady Waddington said sternly. "Truly, I cannot believe it is you speaking thusly. You are generally of a kind nature, and the gentleman was good enough to assist us."

"And insult us," Miss Jeffries returned, recalling the man's highly egotistical manners.

"Ladies, ladies." Sir Henry handed them each a glass of brandy. "Let us drink to . . . to my powder. Good. Now go and refresh yourselves and then you shall give me a proper explanation." The stern note in his voice was not to be disobeyed. Excusing themselves, the pair withdrew to their rooms.

Standing before her looking glass, Elizabeth was forced to smile, then laugh, at the image reflected back. The feathers of her poke bonnet were bent askew and coated with a film of white. Her face was streaked, for she had attempted to rid herself of most of the powder on it. *If it were black, I'd look the proper chimney sweep,* she joked to herself, seeing that the chalk and flour mixture had managed a complete covering. "Why, even my cap . . ." Elizabeth began as she untied her bonnet. Her jaw flexed with the remembrance of the overdressed Frenchman's words about lines coming to her features. Dropping the bonnet to the floor, she stalked to the washbasin and gave her face a thorough scrubbing, then returned to her mirror. Carefully studying her features, she started when she heard someone enter.

"I didn't mean to frighten you, miss," apologized young Martha Spense, who acted as Elizabeth's abigail when she stayed with her uncle. "My, what a . . ."

"An absurd sight," Elizabeth finished for her, laughing. "Come, Spense, unfasten me. You know, I never realized how fortunate we are that powdered hair has gone out of style. I cannot imagine how my uncle tolerates having his done," she said, stepping out of her gown.

" 'Twas fortunate no one was injured," Martha offered, news of the accident having reached belowstairs quickly.

"Yes," her mistress mused, handing her the frilled spinster's cap. "After you lay out my fresh garments, you can take these things away. They need more than a simple washing to save them."

Martha hurried to get new petticoats and a fresh gown from the wardrobe and then slowly picked up the dust-laden garments. Pausing at the door before she left, she gave Miss Jeffries a second glance. Never before had she noticed her mistress give but cursory inspection to her appearance, while all other ladies dawdled hours away. But now she seemed drawn to the looking glass, passing a hand across her cheeks and contemplating herself closely. "I'll be right back, miss," Spense offered, wondering if she should stay, the accident evidently having upset her mistress more than she was allowing.

"Oh, that is all right. I can manage," Elizabeth told her, watching the mirror. Hearing the door close, she gave herself an impulsive grimace. "That's for you, Comte de Cavilon," she said. "Lines on my face, bah. They will come sooner to yours." Her thoughts continued on the comte as she dressed. "It almost seemed," she wondered aloud, "that he recognized me . . . knew me. No," she shook her head, "I must be mistaken." *I would never have forgotten an odious character such as he if I had encountered him before this day,* she thought, leaving her room and walking slowly towards the small salon to join her uncle.

Lady Waddington paused at the door of the salon, struck by a subtle difference in Elizabeth as she sat visiting with her brother.

"Ah, Madeline, now we may hear the whole of this," Sir Henry greeted her, rising. Retaking his seat when she sat, he adjusted his collar and stock. "Elizabeth was telling me that a high-perch phaeton caused your mishap. So many of these young bloods today have no respect for man nor beast when they drive those outlandish vehicles. Why, they aspire to join the Four-in-Hand Club without first learning to master a pony cart, much less highly spirited animals. But I draw us away from our subject." He fidgeted with his waistcoat and cleared his throat. "Pray continue, Elizabeth."

"As I was saying, this young man came too close to us in his phaeton and locked wheels with our coach. Aunt Waddie decided it would be safer for us on the ground"—she looked apologetically at her aunt—"and what with the rocking and jarring the coach was doing as they attempted to right things, she may have been correct."

"And this kind, elegant émigré," Lady Madeline broke in, "was kindly assisting us down, but Elizabeth could not wait until I had introduced myself. She had to step down by herself." While she was speaking Lady Madeline realized what was different about her niece. She was no longer wearing her spinster's cap. What was it the Frenchman had said about it? she wondered.

"If he had not hit me," Elizabeth took up the tale.

"Hit you? 'Pon my soul," Sir Henry exclaimed.

"He didn't hit her. The coach was jerked about the instant she stepped out."

"He hit me and I fell," the young woman insisted.

"That was when the box containing your hair powder came open." Lady Waddington allowed herself a small laugh. "It was such a scene, Henry. This billowing white cloud. Like snow but not nearly as pleasant."

"And he had the nerve to insinuate I should apologize," Elizabeth said, her anger returning.

"If you had not sat upon his lap so long, the comte

could not have said anything to you." Aunt Waddie shook her finger at her niece.

Sir Jeffries shook his head in bewilderment and signaled for silence. "Let us make some sense out of this," he said, rising. "You," he looked at Elizabeth, "you say this man struck you?"

"I suppose it wasn't actually on purpose . . . and not much of a blow," she amended beneath her uncle's something-must-be-done-now glare.

"And you then sat upon his lap . . . in the street?"

"I did not tell him to fall beneath me," she replied defensively.

"The comte was most gracious," Lady Madeline offered. "He tried to catch Elizabeth and didn't say anything about the powder. Not even when she threw what was left of it in his face."

Rolling his eyes, Sir Henry lowered his frame slowly into his chair. "Perhaps it would be best if I did *not* understand the whole of this," he said, looking from his niece to his sister. "Do I dare ask the man's name?"

"A French émigré cannot be of too great a consequence," Elizabeth said in a subdued tone. Her conduct, on the retelling, did not seem as proper as it had at the time.

"He was a very nice gentleman, if somewhat overdressed," her aunt told Sir Henry. "And titled."

"Overdressed, you say?" He rubbed his chin, a new possibility occurring to him. "His name?"

"The Comte de Cavilon," Lady Waddington told him.

"Not Cavilon! You didn't throw hair powder on the

Comte de Cavilon . . . not in the middle of the street . . . in front of others?" Sir Henry demanded of Elizabeth, sitting ramrod straight in his chair.

"You know the comte?" Lady Madeline asked shakily, taken aback by her brother's tone.

"All London knows the man. He is one of the most eligible bachelors in the city, and one of the wealthiest. Oh, Elizabeth, such behaviour . . . and in London."

"I did not know you cared so about . . . society . . . and the power of another's wealth," Elizabeth said, her throat tightening beneath the condemnation she read on her uncle's features.

"It is not his money I care about, dear girl, but his influence in society. Your . . . ways . . ."—he searched for the proper word and failed—"are accepted in Ashford, but here in London I fear . . . The comte could make it deuced uncomfortable for you," he ended weakly.

"I would like to see him try."

"I would not," Sir Henry returned sternly. "You are old enough to know the consequences, Elizabeth. We must make amends." He turned to his sister.

"I will not have you apologizing for me as if I were some . . . some spoiled child." Elizabeth rose, her lip trembling.

"Ahem." A polite cough turned all three's attention to the door.

"These packages just arrived, my lady," Bently announced, motioning to the footman behind him. "This card was with them." He held forth a silver tray.

Lady Madeline picked up the gold-engraved card gingerly, recognizing the parcels as those left behind after the accident. "Take them away," she commanded and turned her eyes to the card. "It is the Comte de Cavilon's." She looked to her brother, then turned it over, dismayed

"What does it say?" Sir Henry asked anxiously.

"I do not know. It is in French. Elizabeth?" She held the card out to her niece.

Taking it, the young woman forced herself to focus on the writing. "His script is as dainty as his lace," she noted.

"But what does it say?" Lady Waddington asked.

"He says . . . says he sends his greetings and hopes that we were not . . . were not unduly 'settled' by the accident." She paused, considering his words. "Oh, don't you see, Aunt, he is making a joke on me."

"Nonsense, it is quite good of him to be concerned."

"Madeline is correct. You are being far too sensitive, Elizabeth," Sir Henry said, his relief apparent. "What has happened to your common sense? I shall have to thank the man for trying to assist you. He is an odd sort, but most speak well of him. Good friend of Tretain's, too. Oh, you recall the Tretains of Southhamptonshire? Home estate is Trees. Well, by the oddest chance I encountered Tretain's wife today." Sir Henry continued with the particulars of the meeting.

His words passed over Elizabeth unheard. *You wanted to be distracted*, she thought, *and you could have come upon no one more different from your rogue than this Comte de Cavilon.* Her conscience nudged her guiltily. *Mayhaps I was a bit unkind. If ever I do meet him again, I shall be more gracious,* Elizabeth mentally promised, turning her attention back to her uncle's story.

"Ah, my dear, you should not be awake at this late hour." Lord Adrian spoke severely as he entered his wife's chambers and found her reading in bed. A smile came to the earl's features as he sat at her side. "But I am glad you are." He kissed her gently. "How are you feeling?"

"Quite well. I found the note you sent rather interesting and had to remain awake until you explained it. What did you mean about the peruke powder?" Lady Juliane asked, reaching up to straighten the collar of his dressing gown.

"That was why I am so late. I took Louis to his rooms. He was quite an awesome sight, completely powdered from peruke to the buckles of his shoes. When he was repaired, we went to White's. The news of the incident had traveled like a fox who hears the hounds draw near, and I knew we would never get away, so I sent the note," Tretain ended, certain the matter was now entirely clear to his wife.

Lady Juliane smiled. "Once more," she said, "only this time begin before you come to the hair powder," she commanded softly.

" . . . That young woman has the manners of a harridan," Lord Adrian ended his second explanation.

"It sounds to me like she had ample provocation for her behaviour," his wife defended the unknown young woman. "I cannot imagine Louis acting in such a reprehensible manner."

"I did think it strange that he tolerated the incident as he did. You know he can get overinvolved with his mannerisms and goad someone who is being too pompous or righteous. Miss Jeffries struck me as neither, but he certainly was baiting her."

"Jeffries? How did you learn her name? It did not sound like proper introductions were made."

"They weren't. I recall wondering how Louis knew her name. He even knew she was a niece to the older woman. I am certain Lady Waddington only had time enough to mention her own name before the fall occurred. Oh, well, Louis has been out of sorts of late and this has cheered him. He seemed much more like himself this eve," Tretain chuckled. "But tell me, what did you do today?"

"I did the shopping I had mentioned, and while I was out I happened to meet Sir Henry Jeffries."

"That's why the woman's name sounded familiar." Tretain snapped his fingers. "Old Sir Henry . . . how is he?"

"Doing very well. He is visiting here with his sister. Brought his niece with him also," Lady Juliane noted, a sly smile coming to her features.

"There is something you are not telling me, Juliane." He eyed her carefully.

"Only that I invited the three of them to our ball next week," she laughed.

"Good, I shall enjoy a visit with Sir Henry."

"Oh, I think it will be very interesting," she continued. "I am especially looking forward to meeting his niece . . . and to seeing you introduce her to Louis."

Tretain cocked his head suspiciously.

"I did neglect to mention the ladies' names, didn't I?" Juliane remarked, attempting to assume a serious air. "They are Lady Waddington . . . and Miss Elizabeth Jeffries."

"Make certain there is no hair powder present," the earl laughed.

"As you wish, my lord." Lady Juliane pursed her lips. "But don't you fear our ball will be dismally dull, then?"

Tretain drew his wife into his arms. "Minx, I wonder if it will be safe to let you attend it," he said gently. "Let us leave Louis to his just deserts . . . and you to yours." His lips claimed hers, his arms tightening about her.

Chapter VIII

The theme of the Tretains' ball, it being on the first May eve, was appropriately that of a May fair. Bunting and streamers of all colours abounded in the grand ballroom. The entire area was ringed with potted tulips, hyacinths, daffodils, and violets, all in full bloom. Large vases of roses stood on pedestals beneath the wall sconces, and boughs of newly leafed oaks completed the sights and aromas of spring.

Lady Juliane had dressed earlier than usual so that she could make one last inspection of the ballroom's decor before the guests arrived. Pausing just inside the huge double doors, she scanned the room. Lady Tretain walked to the center of the room while the footman, who had just finished lighting the many candles in the wall sconces and overhead chandeliers, left. Laying a hand on the gaily painted red-and-white-striped pole, she glided about it, surveying the total effect of the decorations. A smile of satisfaction came over her face. An even brighter smile filled her features when her eyes lit on Lord Adrian.

"My dear," Tretain scolded lightly, "you should be

resting. The evening will be long enough as it is." He approached her slowly, admiringly. "The most beautiful woman in London shall be at my side this eve." He bowed. "A dance, my lady?"

"But there is no music."

"We shall make our own," Lord Adrian said, holding out his arms. Lady Juliane curtsied deeply and accepted his hand. They began to dance slowly about the ballroom. Halfway through the movements of the set they kissed.

"La, such happy domesticity," the Comte de Cavilon's droll voice disturbed them. "Mayhaps there are virtues to the wedded state I have overlooked," he noted with a demure air as he approached them with his peculiar swaying walk.

"'Pon my soul, the man sounds serious." Lady Juliane feigned shock. "I will have to warn all the eligible ladies to beware."

"*Certainement*, if they are as lovely as you." The comte took her hand and kissed it. "*Très belle.*"

"I feel absolutely sinful wearing this." Lady Juliane fingered the sea-blue French silk gown, the material a gift from Cavilon. "Even though you insist it was not smuggled into England."

"I promise you, my lady, it was handled by no common smuggler," Cavilon smiled. "Women," he turned to Tretain. "Why must they be such questioning creatures?"

"That is what makes us interesting," Lady Juliane returned. "And I have a delightful surprise for you this eve." She flashed a large smile.

"Something tells me you had better beware," the earl told Cavilon. "When a woman gets that tone, it can only mean . . ."

"My lord, my lady." Homer stepped into the ballroom. Coaches are arriving."

"To your duties." The comte waved them off. "I shall inspect the wines and make myself *comfortable*."

"You had better . . . while you are able," Tretain tossed over his shoulder as Lady Juliane hurried him from the ballroom.

Lord Adrian and Lady Juliane were respected and liked by the majority of London's *beau monde*. Their social affairs were always well attended, and this eve the crush was even greater than usual. The heat of the many candles, the large number of guests, and the exertions of the dance drove many to the cooler evening air of the veranda, which ran the length of the ballroom's outer wall. The many doors leading to it stood invitingly open, and the Comte de Cavilon led Lady Juliane through one of these at the conclusion of the second set of country dances.

"Your ball is an enviable success," he commented as he led her to a nearby bench. "I have been commanded to see that you rest." The comte motioned for her to sit.

"Truly, I do not feel a bit fatigued." Lady Juliane's eyes strained to see the latecomers entering the ballroom.

"Are you expecting someone of import? Pliny himself?" Cavilon teased.

"I don't believe so," Juliane said, giving him an annoyed frown. But you are certainly dressed to receive royalty this eve," she said, taking in his immaculate white raiment. In the lamplight his appearance was startling but ultimately handsome.

White from his moderately powdered periwig to the silver buckles gleaming on his white cloth-covered shoes, the comte was readily noticeable. The French silk of his jacket and breeches was flawless in fabric and fit, and his sequined wasitcoat was dazzling to the eye. Studying his face, Lady Juliane noticed that he had not used as much powder or rouge as had become his habit. *Why, even his affectations are not as pronounced this eve*, she thought.

"Do you see something amiss?" Cavilon questioned, flicking his kerchief at an imaginary speck on his sleeve.

"Indeed not, my lord Cavilon," she smiled. "You are the best dressed gentleman present . . . but for my husband, of course."

"Why, thank you, my dear," Lord Adrian told his wife, stepping to join them with an older man at his side and a woman of like age upon his arm. "You recall Sir Henry Jeffries. This is his sister, the Marchioness of Waddington, Lady Madeline. My wife, Lady Juliane."

"Most pleased," Lady Waddington smiled. "It was so kind of you to extend an invitation to us, my lady. Elizabeth—" She turned to motion her niece forward and found no one there. "I don't understand," she smiled nervously. "Elizabeth was with us."

"I am happy to learn that Miss Jeffries did come with you." Lady Tretain glanced pointedly at the comte. "I am looking forward to meeting her."

"She is a sweet young woman," Lady Waddington said, also looking to the comte. "My lord Cavilon, I do wish to thank you for your assistance at the time of our mishap. And you also, Lord Tretain. My dear," Lady Madeline turned back to Lady Juliane, "they were such a tremendous aid. I am certain matters would have been far more serious had they not been present."

"Which reminds me," Sir Henry spoke up. "It was not necessary for you to send me a box of peruke powder." His eyes twinkled merrily as he studied Cavilon.

"But of course it was," the comte drawled. "As Lady Waddington says, the matter would have remained serious if we had not been present. I could do no less for the diversion than replace your powder. Let us forget it," he dismissed the subject.

"I told Elizabeth you were a bloody good sport," Sir Henry laughed. "Haven't laughed so much in years," he admitted. "Don't judge the girl too harshly. She tends to fly into the boughs but is a good sort. Bit down of late, worried about her brother and all. Brought her to London to cheer her."

"Poor Elizabeth." Lady Waddington sat beside Lady Juliane. "The most shocking incident happened to her two months past. A villain forced his way into the coach which was bringing the dear girl to my brother. Well, of course, this nearly frightened her to death. Fortunately no harm came to her, but she has been most unsettled ever since." She sighed heavily. "It is most natural for one with her delicate sensibilities."

Tretain, seeing Cavilon surreptitiously scan the ballroom, and noticing his mouth twitching as if fighting off laughter, asked, "Where did this unfortunate incident occur?"

"I do believe I shall try to find Miss Jeffries," Cavilon said before answer could be given. Excusing himself with a flutter of his lace, he gyrated away.

The simple gown Elizabeth was wearing was easily noticeable among the more elaborate dresses of the other women present. Taking two goblets of champagne from a passing footman, the comte headed towards her. When he was but a few paces from his quarry, she saw him. Her jaw clenched determinedly, and she stepped hurriedly away, disappearing in the crush of dancers pausing between sets.

"La, I just knew you ladies were hoping for some refreshment," Cavilon remarked, handing the champagne to two very startled dowagers. "My compliments, my dears," he drawled, bowing exaggeratedly, and moved to follow Miss Jeffries.

Elizabeth, using the skills she had garnered and honed to perfection in evading the suitors set upon her by Sir Henry and Lady Madeline, was successful in keeping from the comte. He himself, hampered because he did not wish to be seen obviously pursuing the lady, paused to consider a course of action. Deep in thought, he stood tapping his cheek impatiently when sudden inspiration dawned. A smile came as he located Miss Jeffries being led into a country set by Tretain.

"Why, my lord Cavilon, isn't this just the most lovely ball yet this season?" A heavy hand halted him as he was about to walk towards the pair. "Lady Tretain has such . . . extraordinary taste. Imagine, a May fair," Lady Reed gushed effusively. "I was just telling my Barbara . . ."

"Ah, Miss Reed." Cavilon bowed with a flourish. "Do you think, Lady Reed, that I might lead your delightful daughter in this set?" he asked, seeking to escape the mother as quickly as possible.

"Oh, my," her ladyship trilled. "My, yes. Off you go," she twittered. Watching them walk away, she preened proudly. "And they said no one could take the Comte de Cavilon's interest."

Miss Reed, however, did not share her mother's delight at this singular honour. Her natural temerity was not aided by the comte's impenetrable manner; he led her through the entire set without a single word. With the last chord of the song fading, she eagerly awaited being returned to her mama and started when, instead, the comte led her across the ballroom. "Let me introduce you to our host, Miss Reed.

"Dear Tretain." Cavilon's voice regained its nasal drawl. "May I present Miss Reed. Miss Reed, the Earl of Tretain, Lord Adrian. I know you have been waiting the opportunity of dancing with Miss Reed, my lord. So happy to oblige you." Cavilon deftly laid the young miss's hand in the earl's and led Miss Jeffries away before a word was said by anyone.

Tretain, recovering from his surprise, turned to Miss Reed and began at once to put her at ease.

"You will honour me with this minuet," Cavilon told Elizabeth, barely glancing at her as they joined the assembling dancers.

"As you wish," she answered, acknowledging this minor defeat graciously, while noting the danger of pausing in the center of a ballroom.

Watching Miss Jeffries unobtrusively while they went through the steps of the formal dance, the comte pondered the reason for his interest and could find no immediate answer. Studying the high-waisted gown of icy green muslin, he found that it neither concealed nor revealed an overly enticing form. He had known others more generously endowed than this country miss. *The color does set off her complexion nicely,* he thought. *Her features are not out of the ordinary. But her eyes, those warm, dark pools of brown, how they sparkle when she is angry.* He sought to condemn but instead discovered more to admire.

Watching the pair from the side, Lady Juliane happily noted Cavilon's interest and found the young woman's disdain for her partner even more diverting. *Mayhaps a wife for dear Louis has been found at last,* she thought. *How perfectly Miss Jeffries' more austere attire and mien complements the brilliance of his wit and toilet.* With this thought she turned to find Lady Waddington. Plotting was in order.

The minuet ending, Cavilon took hold of Elizabeth's arm as he straightened from his bow, preventing her from walking away as she had planned. "You must be frightfully warm," he said solicitously. "Let me take you to the veranda for a touch of fresh air."

"I really do not feel a bit warm, my lord. It must be your French blood," Elizabeth told him cuttingly, feeling her colour rise beneath his unsettling gaze. "But why don't you fetch me an ice," she parried.

They eyed each other appraisingly, as combatants assessing strengths and weaknesses.

Cavilon judged his intention the proper, if more unsettling, ploy to use with this particular female, and put his plan into action immediately. "But I could not bear to be parted from you, even for the short length of time it takes to fetch an ice," he said, daintily sniffing.

Her eyes rose sharply to his.

"You see, my dear, you have quite stolen my heart with your sweet, gentle ways," he continued, fluttering his lace about. "La, but I have shaken your delicate sensibilities." The comte feigned alarm at her continued stare. "This will ease you." He motioned a footman bearing a tray of champagne to their side.

Accepting the goblet calmly, Elizabeth raised it in salute with him. "At your age," she smiled sweetly, "you have come to know life is filled with disappointments."

"You and I," Cavilon ignored her words. "What a delightful match we shall make."

"My lord," Miss Jeffries interrupted him coldly.

"Ah, la, yes, my dear?" The comte waved aside her words. "I know, you wish to go to the veranda with me. You have but to speak to command me. I am your slave," he bowed deeply.

Elizabeth glanced about, seeking to escape, and saw that many were beginning to note their conversation. She suffered Cavilon to lay her hand upon his arm and followed him demurely while she plotted her revenge. "My lord." She halted when they reached an unpopulated area of the veranda. "There is something you must know."

"Speak and I shall obey, *ma chère petite*." He raised her hand to his lips.

"My lord Cavilon," Elizabeth reproved him sharply. "I cannot like your behaviour."

"How lovely you are," he simpered.

Rolling her eyes, Elizabeth decided that tact would never free her. "My lord, I detest, heartily detest, all things French," she told him adamantly.

"But of course," he agreed. "It is only the war, *naturellement*," the comte generously assured her.

"You do not understand." She sought to rein in her rising temper. "It is you, personally, whom I detest."

"La, the English. They make the joke." He waved his lace. "So charming, *ma chère*." Cavilon reached for her hand.

Evading his grasp, Elizabeth turned to walk away and found her elbow in his grip. "My lord, what must I do to be rid of you?" she bit out.

"Smile, *ma petite*, our hostess approaches," the comte told her with killing sweetness.

A madman, Elizabeth thought, staring at him. *He belongs in Bethlehem Hospital—Bedlam.*

"Comte de Cavilon," Lady Juliane teased him with her formality, "who is your lovely partner?"

"Madame Tretain," the comte greeted her, arching

an eyebrow upon seeing that her ladyship was already certain of who was at his side. "May I present Miss Elizabeth Jeffries? Elizabeth, Lady Juliane Tretain."

"My lord, I *dislike* your familiarity," Miss Jeffries said curtly, shaking his hand from her arm. "Pray learn to conduct yourself properly among Englishwomen.

"It has been a pleasure to meet you." She dipped a curtsy to Lady Juliane. "If you will excuse me, I find I must locate my aunt."

"Of course, Miss Jeffries," Lady Tretain murmured. "It must be painful," she took Cavilon's arm as the young lady stiffly walked away, "to be so dreadfully pursued. Just of late I was told by someone who should know that there wasn't a miss in the land who would not fall at your feet. Do you think I should inform Miss Jeffries of this? She doesn't seem to realize it, does she?"

"She will," Cavilon said, his tone causing Lady Juliane to remain deep in thought when he sauntered away.

Chapter IX

"Elizabeth, it is so marvelous," Lady Waddington beamed at her niece. "Henry will be so pleased that you are to be settled at last."

"What are you speaking of, Aunt Waddie?"

"Why, you and the Comte de Cavilon. Everyone is talking of it. To think I had dispaired of you. You are the sly one." She patted Elizabeth's hand, but her rejoicing was quickly tempered by the black look on her niece's face. "Now, Elizabeth . . . what do you mean to do?" A note of fear entered her voice.

"Put that pompous, overdressed French mannikin in his place."

"You can't mean the Comte de Cavilon?" Lady Waddington was aghast at the thought. "Why, he is one of the richest, one of the most eligible men in England," she protested. "You should be grateful that such a man has taken an interest in you . . . at your age. You are *not* going to make a scene, Elizabeth." Aunt Waddie took a firm hold on the other's arm. "Think of Sir Henry, of myself," she implored.

"Am I interrupting?" Lady Juliane hesitated before the pair.

"Nonsense, Lady Tretain, we were merely commenting on what a wonderful time we are having." Lady Madeline managed to swallow her alarm, dropped her hold and smiled pleasantly.

"It is going quite well, isn't it," Lady Juliane smiled in return. "I always fret so about these affairs."

"One in your condition should not be worrying," Lady Waddington told her. "Besides, there is no need. The ball is and *will*," she nudged Elizabeth, "remain flawless."

"Are you enjoying yourself, Miss Jeffries?" Lady Tretain studied the young woman.

Finding she could not disappoint the hopeful expression, Elizabeth searched for an honest compliment. "Yes, the decorations make this as gay as if it were a true May fair, and the music is wonderful."

"I am so glad to hear you say so, for I have a special surprise in which you shall take part a little later this eve." Lady Juliane reached out and took Elizabeth's hand. "But now I would like a coze. You are not taken for this dance?"

"It does not appear that I have to stave off admirers," she replied, laughing lightly.

"Do not fear for that. I believe I know the reason. Lady Waddington, would you excuse us for a few moments?"

"You young people have much to chat about," Lady Madeline smiled approvingly. "Ah, I see Lady Grosvenor. There is a most wicked piece of gossip I hear she is telling." She laughed and sauntered off to accost the lady.

"Let us go to one of the side rooms," her ladyship

suggested. "I have been commanded to rest for a time. Oh, there is no need for concern," she assured the other. "Lord Adrian knows I am not overly fond of dancing and seeks to rescue me through this ploy."

The two women exchanged pleasantries as they walked along. Elizabeth could not help taking an instant liking to Lady Tretain and admiring her simplicity and genuineness. Few women, she was certain, would speak of their families with Lady Juliane's honest affection. When her ladyship broached the subject of Cavilon, however, Elizabeth bridled.

"I am so pleased that Louis has at last found someone. The Comte de Cavilon," Lady Juliane added, seeing the question on the other.

"I must protest, my lady. The Comte de Cavilon has only been amusing himself with his senseless chatter. I have not encouraged him. Quite to the contrary, I have seen him only once prior to this eve and tonight have told him of my dislike of his person."

"And he continues to ignore your words?" Lady Juliane questioned softly, wondering at the young woman's vehemence.

"He has been most obtuse. It must be his French blood." Elizabeth scowled.

"You have a . . . a dislike of the French?"

"I can see no reason not to. My cousin was killed at Quiberon because of the émigrés neglect, and my brother is a prisoner," she explained. "My father would not have died but for his worry over Morton."

"I am so sorry," Lady Tretain said with genuine feeling. "But the Comte de Cavilon does not support Napoleon."

"It makes no difference. He is still French."

"Are you not being a bit harsh?" Lady Juliane asked gently. "Would it not be better to judge each person on his particular merits instead of condemning him because of his country? Louis lost all his lands and some members of his family in the revolution. He dislikes Napoleon as much as any of us," she offered, hoping to ease the other's attitude.

"He does not seem to have suffered from the loss," Elizabeth retorted before she could halt the words.

"If you are wise, Miss Jeffries, you will look beyond Louis' affectations. Many of us wear a mask to protect ourselves from further hurt. But I must rejoin my guests." She rose and held out her hand. "I do wish to be your friend."

"And I yours." Elizabeth accepted the hand, smiling.

"Then you must call on me."

"Gladly. I have few acquaintances in London."

The two walked back towards the ballroom. Lady Juliane pondered on what she had learned and crossed her fingers in the folds of her gown, fervently hoping that what she had planned for Louis and Miss Jeffries did not erupt into a scene. Excusing herself when they reached the ballroom, she hurried away to find Cavilon.

"Would you consider pleasing an aging gentleman by consenting to this dance?" Sir Henry bowed before his niece.

"As long as you promise not to tread on my toes," she laughed, accepting his hand.

When the piece ended, Sir Henry kept her hand in his when they left the set. "I am very proud of you," he said, the happy gleam in his eye causing Elizabeth's heart to sink upon realizing the probable cause for his words. "I knew you wouldn't disappoint me, my dear."

A fanfare sounded before she could speak. *I must tell him later*, she thought, turning to see what was happening. *I will explain this mistake. Drat the comte!* Elizabeth tapped her foot angrily, her heart heavy at having to disappoint her uncle, who had always given her love, asking nothing in return.

A second fanfare sounded, presenting Lord and Lady Tretain in the center of the ballroom near the Maypole. The guests ceased chattering.

"No May fair would be complete without the dance of the Maypole," Lord Adrian announced.

A twitter ran through the company. Those familiar with the country May fairs recalled the wild exuberances done in honour of spring.

"Since it isn't possible for all of us to take part, we have drawn names . . . carefully," Tretain continued. "The footmen will now escort the gentlemen who have been chosen."

Laughter and mild joking abounded as everyone strained to see whom the footmen were approaching. Applause and good-natured teasing followed many of the dozen gentlemen brought to the center. Selection had been careful indeed, and the well-known members among the dozen were indicative of the Tretains' popularity. The Beau, George Brummell, whose gracious consent forced the more serious Lord Petersham to follow his lead, was a close friend of the Prince of Wales. Lord Addington, soon to be prime minister, joined them, along with some of the younger members of the *ton*. Last to be selected was the Comte de Cavilon.

"And now"—Lady Juliane signaled for the footmen to return to the guests surrounding the center of the ballroom—"the ladies."

There was little surprise as Countess Levien and Lady Jersey were led forth. A murmur of approval rose as Lady Addington and Lady Petersham joined their husbands, and a polite spattering of applause heralded the choice of young Miss Seymour, who blushingly joined her fiancé. A gabble of whispering arose when the footman halted before Miss Jeffries.

A cold chill swept through Elizabeth when the footman bowed before her. Hurriedly she looked to Lady Juliane, but her hostess was busily occupied positioning the ladies beside the gentlemen and keeping the more doubtful of her selected dancers from bolting.

"Go on," Sir Henry whispered, giving her a small nudge. "Show them you are equal to any London miss."

To go forward was to give further credence to the gossip about herself and Cavilon. To refuse would be to embarrass her uncle beyond redemption. Swallowing the lump in her throat, Elizabeth allowed the footman to lead her to Lord Adrian.

"There is nothing to fear, Miss Jeffries," Tretain assured her, misreading her look. "Simply follow the other ladies' steps." He took her hand and led her to her place.

A sigh of relief came when Elizabeth saw that she was nowhere near the comte.

"Remember, when the signal is given you must begin to weave with the person you are next to, instead of with the pole. When the end of the streamers is reached in each pair, we shall complete the pole," Lady Juliane whispered hurriedly as she placed the bright-coloured streamer in Elizabeth's hand.

The Tretains took their places; the music was struck. Six and twenty dancers began to move out from the Maypole, halting when the streamers were taut. Lord Adrian began the circular weaving pattern that characterized the dance. The pace increased. Enthusiasm and laughter infected the dancers, and Elizabeth found that she was enjoying herself. Even Cavilon was not totally scorned as they occasionally wove past one another.

The signal was given, and laughter-filled confusion followed as choices as to who was nearest were hurriedly made. Seeing the gentleman before her taken, Elizabeth turned and, with sinking heart, saw the Comte de Cavilon moving towards her. Their streamers gradually shortened, then Cavilon's hand was upon hers and his arm circled her waist.

With each individual pair thus united, the final weaving began about the Maypole, drawing the dancers ever closer to it.

The arm about her waist had far more strength in it than Elizabeth had thought possible for one of the comte's mien. His hand upon hers was gently firm.

Glancing over her shoulder into his eyes, she felt an odd sensation flow through her. His wrist against hers, their pulses beat in unison. For a brief moment his eyes spoke an appeal. She quickly averted her own. Daring to glance once more, Elizabeth encountered the languid, bored expression previously present.

The music was near its end, and the dancers were moving with increasing speed. Because of their closeness to each other, great care was taken not to jostle anyone too roughly. Lord Petersham, just in front of Elizabeth, stumbled on his wife's skirt, and only Cavilon's deft movement and strength saved Elizabeth from falling over them. The streamers' ends were reached at that moment, and the crowd poured onto the ballroom floor as the orchestra went immediately into a lively country set.

Bemused, Elizabeth found the comte's arm still about her as they moved from the floor onto the veranda. Her dislike and anger were forgotten in the comforting security of his hold. But the magic moment passed as quickly as it had descended upon her, and Cavilon again became the effeminate fop, daintily mopping his brow. "I do hope," he took his arm from her waist, "that you are not fond of such personal contact, my dear. I do find such gestures tiresome. But of course, you English are so sensible about such matters," he drawled with assurance. "I must take my leave now, *ma petite*. I shall call upon your uncle in the morn." Brushing the startled young woman's hand with a kiss, he sauntered away, his shoulder dipping with each step, his lace aflutter.

Lady Waddington rushed to her niece's side. "What did he say?" she asked excitedly.

"He is going to call upon Uncle in the morn," Elizabeth managed, anger and mirth struggling within her for supremacy. "I don't believe that . . . man," she ended hopelessly. "Could we not go, Aunt? I find I have a beastly headache."

"Wait here while I find Sir Henry," Aunt Waddie told her solicitously. "Just too much excitement, my dear," she assured her before hurrying away.

Elizabeth stepped to the balustrade surrounding the veranda and gazed at the crescent moon above. Thinking of Cavilon's pompous assurance, she felt like screaming out her protest, her denial. *The man is odious, detestable in looks and obnoxious in manner,* she told herself. *He cannot possibly mean to make an offer for my hand.*

She bit her lip; the memory of the tall, dark unknown Englishman flashed to mind. Cavilon could not compare even if, for a moment, there had been a feeling of . . . Elizabeth pushed the thought aside. He was French; she could never marry him. Marriage to him would be a mockery. Uncle Henry would have to be disappointed. Suddenly Elizabeth felt tears begin to well. What had happened to her sane, orderly spinster's existence?

Chapter X

The morning after the ball Lord Tretain received a secretive visitor with whom he was closeted for over an hour. When the man left, the earl ordered his landau and headed for Cavilon's apartments. Learning that the comte had not returned home since the eve before, he went to White's.

The doorman at the club greeted him cheerfully and directed him to the hazard room.

With a nod, Tretain hurriedly strode forward. Cavilon used gambling much as other men used drink. That he was disturbed enough to remain all night at the hazard table did not speak well for the earl's intention. Pausing in the doorway, Tretain's eyes swept the room. At this early hour only one table was occupied, and two of the gentlemen at it were rising. The earl nodded as they walked past. A third rose drunkenly.

"My solicitor shall call upon you, Lord Tenbury," Cavilon drawled disinterestedly.

Tenbury snorted angrily and stumbled away.

"It had been a long evening," Tretain said, walking to the table and sitting down. "Successful, I see." He waved at the pile of coin and notes on the table. "I am always amazed"—the earl leaned back, studying the comte closely—"how you always appear as fresh in the twelfth hour as you did in the first."

"The mark of the true gentleman." Cavilon flicked a speck from his white silk jacket. "Do remove this," he ordered a footman, waving at the coins. "And bring a bottle of your best Warre port."

"You are in a black temper," Tretain noted warily, knowing that Cavilon considered port the basest of wines, preferring the better French varieties, which his work allowed him to procure in spite of the war.

"You certainly are out early this morn. I would think you would be resting," Cavilon commented and turned his gaze on the earl.

"Gilreaux called on me this morn."

"That is of no interest to me." The comte sipped at the port placed before him, his movements elaborately exaggerated.

"Someone must go. . . ."

"Not I." Cavilon fluttered his kerchief.

"Listen." Tretain hunched over the table, glancing about to see if anyone was near. "Melas has Masséna besieged in Genoa. Bonaparte has sent Moreau to attack Krug's Austrian divisions, and there are runners leaving Paris daily with orders to procure supplies and transportation along a line from Dijon to Villeneuve to St. Pierre. He means to defeat Melas and take all of northern Italy. Someone must go to Paris and . . ."

"Did you not hear me? I shall not. There are others who can do what is wished."

The earl sat back and studied his friend. "What is it, Louis?"

"You yourself once told me a man is good at this work only so long as his concentration holds, as long as he has no other interest. *N'est-ce pas?*"

Tretain nodded slowly.

"I find myself distracted." The drawl was gone from the comte's voice. "You see, there is a difference in changing poses consciously, and in reverting unconsciously. The former may save one's life, while the latter will surely end it. Last eve I lost that fine line of control."

"So your affectations were not as pronounced as usual. No one noticed," the earl objected.

"You did." He had made his point. "But it is not that which concerns me. Later, when I was alone with Miss Jeffries, for a moment I almost became Martin."

"Then she is the woman whose coach you used to get out of Folkestone." Understanding dawned.

"*Oui.* She has the oddest effect upon me. I feel compelled to pursue her and yet driven to escape," Cavilon said slowly.

"Then you have your answer. She could not follow you to France."

Cavilon shook his head. Slowly the shoulder tipped; he fluttered his lace. "It is too late. I am to call upon Sir Henry Jeffries in two hours."

The surprise he felt did not show on Tretain's schooled features. "Will she have you?" he asked, thinking of his wife's words.

"But who would not?" The comte rose with a flourish. "I must go and prepare myself." He bowed and gyrated from the room.

"A fine time for him to fall in love," Tretain murmured, rising. *Mayhaps he shall be disappointed*, he thought, for Juliane did not hold the union likely without a great deal of persuasion on Louis' part and of a different tack than he had begun. *Perhaps the mission could be delayed*, Tretain continued thoughtfully. *Miss Jeffries' behaviour last eve was not that of a love-struck miss. But then, again Louis is not the ordinary suitor.* He shrugged and decided he had better make arrangements for someone else to go to France.

Elizabeth paced nervously as she awaited her uncle in his office. After tossing and turning all night, she had decided to speak with him about the Comte de Cavilon.

"Good morn, my dear," Sir Henry greeted her cheerfully and sat behind his desk. "Sit down now. Be comfortable." He chuckled. "No reason to be so serious. This is a day for rejoicing."

Oh, Uncle, she sighed to herself. Her spirits sank, looking at his beaming smile. Her eyes traveled to his powdered peruke, then down to the old-fashioned frock coat and the stock. A feeling of helplessness gradually descended upon Elizabeth. Sir Henry's thinking on marriage was as antiquated as his toilet.

"Come, come. Let's have a smile. I had a note from the Comte de Cavilon early this morn. He shall be calling in an hour," Sir Henry told her, looking at his timepiece.

If Cavilon meant to call, she was left no choice.

"That is why I must speak with you, Uncle," Elizabeth began slowly.

"No need. No need at all. I will be delighted to see a dowry is given. And never fear, there shall be a decent sum settled upon you," he assured her.

Distress filled her features. "Uncle Henry, I do not wish to marry the Comte de Cavilon. In fact, I shall refuse to do so."

Sir Jeffries stiffened. "You are not a green miss, Elizabeth. This maidenly reserve is out of place. The comte's title may not be English, but he is from an old aristocratic family. This nonsense about your feelings against the French is for children. He will provide for you much better than I shall be able to. You know that my property must go to Morton when I die," Sir Henry told her evenly.

"I mean to refuse him if he offers." She studied the white knuckles of her clenched hands.

"That would be most foolhardy. It saddens me greatly to think you so shortsighted."

"Uncle, I know you wish me to be happy. Please do not insist upon this marriage," Elizabeth pleaded softly.

Studying his niece closely, Sir Henry debated what to do. He did wish her happiness but firmly believed a financially secure marriage would achieve it. "Could we not arrange a period of courtship before you decide so irrevocably?" he offered. "You have known the comte for so short a time. If you dealt together for a longer space, you might come to see that he has many amenable qualities," Sir Henry said more hopefully, unwilling to see the match slip by.

"If . . . if I would agree to this . . . this courtship, within a set time, and if at the end of the period I still found the idea of attachment with Lord Cavilon . . . distasteful, would you agree I need not marry him?" she questioned.

"But of course, my dear." Sir Henry rose with a sigh of relief. Drawing Elizabeth to her feet, he brushed her cheek with a kiss. "You are of age, my dear. No one can force you, nor do we wish to. Now take that dire look off your face." He pinched her cheek. "Why don't you take Spense and go shopping or whatever it is you women do to cheer up. I shall arrange the matter with the Comte de Cavilon," he told her, leading her to the door. "It shall be for the best."

I can't blame Elizabeth for her hesitancy, Sir Henry thought as he stared at the figure in sky-blue satin seated before him. *Shan't like to be tied to the likes of him. Never did care for popinjays who powder their faces.* He noted Cavilon's whitish cheeks and lightly rouged lips. *Wonder what sort of man he is behind all that folderol.* Doubt crept into Sir Henry's thoughts. He resolutely pushed it aside. His niece must be cared for, and a husband was the only proper way to assure her future, he told himself. *'Tis unfortunate the comte is the only one to have ever reached the stage of actually offering for her hand.* He smiled. The fact that Cavilon had dealt with Elizabeth and was still offering for her showed a degree of determination that could not be scoffed at.

Beneath the older man's smile Cavilon felt an inner unease. This proposal made perfect sense last eve in the midst of battling with Miss Jeffries, but it had lost relevancy in the harsh light of morn. He crossed his legs and drew a lace scarf from his heavily embroidered waistcoat.

"And what may I do for you?" Sir Henry felt the moment opportune to begin the interview.

"It is such a . . . delicate matter." The comte fluttered the scarf nervously. "And I but so recently come to your acquaintanceship. I fear you shall think me too bold in what I wish to say."

"Let me assure you your fears are groundless." Sir Henry cleared his throat and drummed his fingers on his desk top. "I believe you mean to speak of my niece, Miss Jeffries," he forced the point.

"Ah, Miss Jeffries. The most beautiful mademoiselle I have ever beheld." Cavilon clasped his hands to his heart. "She has stolen my affections. I think only of her." He sniffed daintily. "Of course, Sir Henry, you as a man realize that one cannot permit such a condition to be unattended. It interferes so with important matters. Therefore I have decided it would be best to wed Miss Elizabeth. One's wife never . . . Well, one's wife is simply one's wife." He fluttered his scarf. "I am prepared to settle a handsome amount upon Elizabeth when we marry. Would ten thousand pounds be agreeable?" he asked with an air of boredom, in reality studying Sir Jeffries keenly from behind his drooping eyelids.

A large smile came to the older man. The sum named was outrageously generous. Sir Henry chose his words carefully. "That is *most* generous, my lord. There is one *minor* detail which we must attend to first, however. Elizabeth has spent the majority of her life in Folkestone, living in a very quiet manner. She has been properly educated and will prove a most acceptable hostess, skilled in all the social affairs," he hastened to assure the comte. "But since she has been so sheltered, she is of a retiring nature and is naturally sensitive, showing, of course, that she is of genteel quality. It will therefore, I think, be most wise if there be a period of courtship, a time in which you may both come to know each other better. In this way Elizabeth's shyness can be naturally overcome."

"Miss Jeffries does not wish to wed me?" Cavilon drawled with a hint of offense in his voice.

"Oh, no. No," Sir Henry blustered. "While Elizabeth is not a . . . not just from the schoolroom, she is rather green in the area of . . . of men. Well, I am certain you understand," he ended hopefully.

"This courtship you propose, how long is it to be?" Cavilon rapped his chin contemplatively.

"Could we not say three months?"

"I have no objections to this." The comte rose and placed a limp hand in Sir Henry's outstretched palm. "I wish to see Elizabeth now."

"Mayhaps you could dine with us this eve? My niece has gone shopping this morn," Sir Jeffries explained.

"With Lady Waddington?"

"I believe she took her abigail."

"Then I must be content to see her this eve. We shall conclude the business portion of the marriage when the wedding date is named, *n'est-ce pas?*"

"That will do very well, my lord. I shall see you to the door."

The two men discussed the present state of the war as they walked through the corridor. Coming into the main entry, they saw a young woman on the upper landing.

"Why Spense, has Miss Jeffries stayed at home?"

"No, sir. She said she was going out for a short time," answered the abigail, bobbing a quick curtsy.

"Then Lady Madeline accompanied her," Sir Henry assured Cavilon.

"Oh, no sir. Miss Jeffries went alone." Martha offered. "She said she wanted to think some matters through."

"Do you know her direction?" Cavilon questioned without bothering to look at the young woman.

"Miss has shown a preference for St. James's Park, my lord."

"*Merci*. I shall go there at once, Sir Henry. It shall not do to have my future bride seen unchaperoned. I trust that in the future she will not go about unattended," the comte stated as he carefully arranged his lace scarf.

"Of course not, my lord," he was quickly assured.

"My wife must be most proper in all matters, at all times," Cavilon admonished, his voice rising. With a flutter of his hand, he withdrew.

"It will take a miracle," Sir Henry muttered, mopping his brow, "for this match to be achieved."

Chapter XI

The brilliant sunshine and May fragrance of green grass and blooming flowers did little to cheer Elizabeth as she sat upon a bench in St. James's Park.

Why, she thought, *does my mind keep turning back to the rogue? I know nothing of him. I would not even recognize him, and yet he comes unbidden into my thoughts each day. You are too old for such foolishness,* she scolded herself, and began sermonizing, reciting the catechism of reasons Aunt Waddie and Uncle Henry were certain to batter her with in regard to the comte.

Cavilon, she mused. Even he had moved her, if only for a moment on the eve just past. Was there something wrong with her that her heart could be tugged about? *You cannot despise a man and love him,* she admonished herself. *And you cannot love a man you know nothing about,* her subconscious responded. She sighed heavily. Her only hope was that Cavilon would reconsider and find her unattractive, if not distasteful, when viewed as a prospective bride.

Rising, Elizabeth began to walk, dwelling on what

she might do to dissuade the comte without severely embarrassing her uncle.

Sonething solid brushed against the back of her skirt, causing Elizabeth to spin around. Looking down, she saw one of the largest, woolliest dogs she had ever laid eyes on. He sat down and whined imploringly.

"Why, are you hungry?" she asked.

Two loud barks answered her question.

She reached out and patted his grey coat, bringing a puff of dust to the air. "Where is your master?" Elizabeth glanced about but could see no one paying any attention to the beast. "I suppose I could buy you a loaf," she mused, and began walking towards the street where vendors hawked wares of every conceivable sort. Buying a loaf, she tore a piece from it and tossed it to the dog.

The animal had stayed a short distance from the vendor's cart and now bounded forward to catch the bread, swallowing the piece in one gulp.

"My, you are hungry," Elizabeth laughed, tossing another hunk. Walking slowly, she turned back towards the center of the park. The dog ran before her, circling about her, pausing to bow down before her every few paces and beg another piece.

The Comte de Cavilon had seen Elizabeth at the vendor's cart and ordered his coach to halt. A smile came to his lips as he watched her play with the huge dog. With a command for his coachmen to wait, he stepped down and slowly gyrated towards her.

Tossing the last piece of bread, Elizabeth laughed

at the dog still prancing about her barking. "That is all there is," she told him, holding out her empty hands as proof.

A sharp gasp replaced the laughter, for a low growl came from the huge beast. Suddenly he leapt at her but, instead of attacking, he sank his teeth into her reticule, which hung from her wrist by two cords. A tug of war ensued.

"Let go of it," Elizabeth snapped, but was unsuccessful. The large dog shook its head, throwing her off balance, and came away with the reticule in its jaws, bounding towards a clump of shrubbery in the distance.

When Cavilon saw the dog lunge, he, too, thought Elizabeth was being attacked. Dropping all affectation, the comte sprinted towards her. When the dog loped off with the reticule dangling in its jaw, he realized what was happening and slowed his steps. A chuckle escaped when Elizabeth gave chase to the beast.

The dog disappeared into the shrubbery with Miss Jeffries entering on its heels. Shouts and cries as well as vociferous barking bespoke an encounter involving more than the young woman and the animal.

Easing his way through the shrubs, a bark of laughter came from Cavilon at the scene before him. The dog's master, a young lad of ten or eleven, had been snared by Elizabeth. She was attempting to regain possession of her reticule while the dog nipped at her ankles and pawed at her skirt. In desperation she pushed the lad to the ground and fell upon him. The huge woolly dog followed suit and jumped astride Elizabeth, lying down across her back and effectively pinning her.

"Get off me," the lad complained. "Ye be crushin' the very life from me."

"Order your beast from my back," Elizabeth retorted angrily. "And let go of my reticule. What do you mean by sending this monster against poor defenseless women?" she demanded, twisting about and trying to push the dog off.

The huge beast yawned, ignoring her efforts, and laid its head upon its gigantic paws.

Ceasing the struggle for a moment, Elizabeth looked straight ahead and saw an immaculate pair of white silk hose. Her eyes traveled up past sky-blue satin breeches.

"Sir, please remove this animal . . ." Her words ended before the sentence was finished. "My Lord Cavilon," she murmured, her heart sinking.

"La, my dear." He daubed at his forehead with his kerchief. "I am quite fatigued by the walk. I do seem to encounter you in the most unusual places and in the most extraordinary poses."

"Would you please find someone who would be able to help me? These are a pair of thieves." Elizabeth tried to control the anger she felt welling within her.

"Rather, *ma petite*, I would say they have you," Cavilon returned with a flutter of his hand at her predicament.

"When I am free"—Elizabeth's eyes threw daggers—"you had best be gone. Never depend upon a Frenchman for aid," she gritted through her clenched teeth.

The comte ignored her words and spoke to the lad. "Your beast is well trained?"

"His name be Barney," the boy snorted.

"He will do whatever you command him, *n'est-ce pas?*"

"Aye."

"This," Cavilon tossed a guinea in the air and caught it, "is yours if he removes himself from the mademoiselle."

"Up, Barney," the boy commanded, and the dog rose and stepped to one side. Yawning widely, it sat down on the grass.

"*Ma petite* does not yet obey my commands so well"—the comte tapped his cheek contemplatively—"but I believe she will rise if you surrender the reticule."

The boy did so grudgingly. Elizabeth knelt, keeping one hand on his arm.

"Ye said she'd let me be," the lad complained.

"*Non*, I said she does not yet obey me." Cavilon shrugged nonchalantly. "Do you wish the boy taken to Newgate?" he asked Elizabeth.

"Newgate? But there are many vile men there, thieves and murderers," she said, struggling to her feet, a glowering look covering her features when Cavilon failed to assist her. "Thank you," she said sarcastically, brushing at her skirt.

"But I could not soil my gloves," Cavilon protested innocently. "As for the lad, he is a thief also."

"Where are your parents?" Elizabeth questioned the ragged lad.

"Me be an orphan. But Barney takes good care o' me. We eats well, we do," he assured her.

"What is your name?" Her resolve to see him punished began to melt beneath his large-blue-eyed gaze.

"Tom. It's all I'm known as," he shrugged.

"And no one has ever looked after you?"

"Me told ye, Barney does," Tom protested.

"You live by stealing," she said condemningly.

" 'Tis common, Miss Jeffries," the comte interrupted. "There are many such as this in London. Would you have them starve? Prison will be best for the lad."

"I do not need your suggestions, my lord," she snapped.

"Ah, my dear, but I do think you need my assistance. What will your aunt and uncle say if you walk through the streets of London looking as you do?"

Elizabeth took in her stained and torn gown. A silent curse acknowledged him correct.

"I will have one of my footmen take the boy away," he told her.

"What of me Barney?" Tom wailed.

"Hush," Elizabeth commanded. "You are both coming home with me."

Cavilon arched his brow.

"Have your coach brought forward," she ordered.

"Only because I am a gentleman." He bowed elaborately and minced back through the shrubs.

"Coo, me ain't never seen none the likes o' him," Tom told her as they waited. "Ain't he pretty, mum?"

"To some, I suppose," she snapped, and pulled the lad after her.

Signaling the footman to open the coach door, the

comte stood to one side as Elizabeth prodded Tom inside and then was herself assisted by the footman.

Barney, seeing his master disappear in front of the young woman, plunged into the coach just as Elizabeth stepped inside. She found herself pushed aside as the dog clambered onto the seat beside Tom.

Picking herself up, she decided it would be easier to sit across from the pair after all, and she slid over as Cavilon gingerly joined them.

"The coach will have to be entirely redone," he sniffed, raising his kerchief to his nose to cover the odor from the pair opposite. "I see that marriage with you shall be quite . . . expensive, *ma petite* . . . but vastly interesting."

A storm erupted when the foursome entered Lady Waddington's home a short while later. The unfortunate mistress of the house was preparing to depart when they entered and was promptly knocked down by Barney's exuberant greeting. Her shrieks brought Sir Henry and the servants running to the scene, and sheer pandemonium broke loose as Tom was chased by the footmen, who in turn were pursued by Barney.

Cavilon deftly drew Elizabeth from the midst of the fray. Raising her hand to his lips, he brushed it with a kiss. "I shall take my leave *ma chère petite* . . . until a more appropriate time. With your delicate sensibilities, for your uncle has assured me they are most properly delicate, you will require some time to recover from these"—his hand encompassed the mad scene before them—"exuberances. I shall call to take you riding tomorrow afternoon. We must, after all, begin our courtship." A teasing twinkle appeared in his eye and was gone just as quickly. Before she could prevent it, he leaned forward and kissed her, then was fluttering and prancing away, leaving her looking after him in confusion.

"Elizabeth!" Sir Henry's roar broke through the spell that held her.

Dashing into the fray, she intercepted Tom and was again felled by Barney.

"Take that . . . that beast to the mews," Sir Henry commanded the footman, who was struggling to keep a hold on the huge dog.

"Tell Barney to go with them," Elizabeth told Tom. "It will be all right."

"Go on, Barney," the lad said sorrowfully.

"Take him to the kitchen and have him scrubbed," Sir Henry continued his orders. "Madeline, you can stop that confounded fainting. The beast is gone. Elizabeth, to your room at once. When you have repaired your appearance, you will come to my office and explain this."

"Yes, Uncle," she said and hurried up the stairs.

"I will check with the authorities," Sir Henry told Elizabeth at the conclusion of her explanation. "If the boy is indeed an orphan, a place shall be found for him at my home in Ashford."

"And Barney . . . the dog?" she added.

"The beast can come, but only if it is well controlled," her uncle grudgingly granted.

"Oh, thank you. I am certain Tom can do that." Elizabeth rose with a grateful smile on her lips.

"We are not finished, miss." Sir Henry pointed for her to retake her seat. "I am certain that your description of the encounter with the lad and his dog has been altered somewhat in the telling to put everyone in the best light possible. The condition of your toilet upon your return, however, I feel is ample proof of what must have occurred." Her objection was rendered useless. "What concerns me is that you made no mention of the Comte de Cavilon assisting you, other than to convey you and your acquisitions home. Am I correct in assuming that he was present when the animal stole your reticule?"

"But I did not say that Barney . . ."

"I know London's ways, my girl. The folderol you told me about the boy makes a good story, but that is not my worry at the present moment. Simply answer the question," he told her curtly.

Elizabeth nodded slowly.

"And the comte did nothing to seize the lad?" Sir Henry continued his questioning.

"The comte did . . ." Elizabeth hesitated, uncertain of her uncle's intent, and discovered that she had no wish to have Cavilon appear negligent in the matter.

"Well?" her uncle prompted.

"He paid the lad to . . . to come along with me," she finished weakly.

"And yet you permitted him to kiss you? Yes, my dear, I saw that. I am not blind from old age yet. I take it then, that despite all you have said, you have consented to wed him?"

"The Comte de Cavilon and I did not discuss marriage," she answered. The sinking feeling which came over her vied with the realization that she had forgotten that Cavilon was French. "If we had, I would not have accepted him," she finished irresolutely.

"And yet you allowed him to kiss you?" Sir Henry snorted. "With all the servants to see?"

"Considering Barney's presence, I hardly think they were watching, Uncle," Elizabeth tried to joke.

"This will not do at all."

"But I—"

"Silence. I must think." Sir Henry rose and paced back and forth, his features becoming sterner with each step. It was one thing to wed Elizabeth to a foppish man, quite another to wed her to a womanly coward who would not protect her from a thieving lad. Cavilon, for all his wealth, could only be a scoundrel to let a beast such as Barney accost his future wife and lift no finger to help her. It was a base man who would not aid a genteel woman and yet took personal liberties with her. His thoughts came hard and fast. *The comte may be wealthy, but there are fates worse than poverty*, he concluded, and marriage to that effeminate coward would be the worst for a proud young woman like his niece. "I want you to go and pack, Elizabeth," Sir Henry announced. "Madeline shall go with you to Ashford. You may take the lad—what was his name . . . Tom. You will depart in the morn. There will be no marriage between you and the Comte de Cavilon, and it would be best if you were gone from London for a time in the event the man proves difficult in the matter. Mayhaps we can return in the fall."

"As you wish, Uncle Henry." Elizabeth rose and

walked slowly to the door. "Will you come with us?" she asked, looking back.

"I must call on the comte and tell him of the refusal. There is also the matter of the lad, which I will see to personally. Then I shall join you."

"Thank you . . . for taking Tom in," she murmured, and left, quietly closing the door behind her. She knew her heart should be singing for joy, her freedom from Cavilon a fact. *That was what you wished*, she told herself. Why then, Elizabeth pondered, did she feel this peculiar emptiness? Why did she wish to cry more than laugh?

Chapter XII

"Was that Sir Henry I saw leaving?" Tretain asked Cavilon as he joined the comte in his study.

"It was," the other returned cryptically.

"What could he have said to raise your bile so?" the earl asked, seeing the lace scarf which lay before Cavilon on the desk was torn in two.

"Sir Henry Jeffries has regretfully informed me that my offer for his niece's hand has been refused. My . . . person has been found . . . undesirable. Damn the man. He so much as called me a coward." Cavilon's eyes narrowed in frustrated anger. "Elizabeth is being sent to Ashford."

"It may be for the best," Tretain said softly. "Even you could not say she was amenable to the match."

"If I recall correctly, Lady Juliane's feelings before your marriage were much the same as Elizabeth's, and that did nothing to alter your pursuit," Cavilon noted coldly. "But then, you did not have this," he threw the torn lace to the floor, "to compete against."

"A true love would have seen through your affectations."

"In three meetings I am to overcome this?" The

comte's gesture indicated his powdered and laced appearance.

"Perhaps it is just Sir Henry's old-fashioned ideas about what denotes a man that have led to this and it has nothing to do with Elizabeth," Tretain began.

"There is more to it than that. Yesterday my wealth was enough excuse for my overelaborate, foppish mannerisms."

"Then you should rejoice that the girl did not accept you."

Cavilon scowled at Tretain. "I know you mean well, but . . ." he sighed heavily, "I love her. The moment I thought Barney was lunging for her, I knew it for a certainty."

The earl cocked his head questioningly.

"Barney is a four-footed giant fond of relieving ladies of their reticules," the comte half explained.

"I see." Tretain's interest grew.

The comte's face had darkened, his thoughts far from the incident in St. James's Park. "I wanted to win her love in spite of my present guise. If she accepted me in this state, I would know it was from affection."

"How could you have been certain?" the earl questioned slowly. "Your wealth is a great temptation to many. Think of all the plotting mamas and widows upon whom you have used your skills of avoidance these ten years past, if not since you stepped into your first pair of breeches. When love is genuine, you will know it," he ended earnestly, the distress he saw on his friend's face troubling him deeply.

"There are so few women of honour, of principle. Some are lured by money, some by a handsome face."

A deep bitterness had come into Cavilon's voice. "They swear to love forever but stay only while the jewels and money last. They promise to wed, then fly into another man's arms the moment the first is from their side. How does one recognize this genuineness you speak of?

"Once I loved and was loved," the comte continued, "or so I believed. You should have heard the vows we swore to one another, the promises we made. But her words meant nothing." His fist came down on the desk with bruising force. "She betrayed me. I was gone but two weeks and on returning found her wed to another, who had already come into his inheritance and did not have a father standing in the way of his fortune, as I did. Not a word would she say; she laughed at my protest. I had believed her pure and innocent, and thus learned a lesson about women I have never forgotten."

Tretain stared at his hands. There was nothing he could say to relieve such a deep wound.

"In Elizabeth Jeffries I thought to find a woman who would honour any promise she made. Had she wed me even when she loathed me, I would have known then that if I could capture her heart, she would love me always, that she would never play me false."

"But I did not realize that an agreement had been reached between you," Tretain noted, puzzled.

"There was none." The question broke Cavilon's brooding. "There was none," he repeated, a studied expression easing his dark look.

"Had you not thought to purchase land in an eastern shire?" the earl asked. "Perhaps you could spend some time with Lord Tenbury. I believe his lands lie near Ashford." Tretain grinned.

"Mayhaps." A challenging gleam came to the comte's eyes.

"Wasn't that Tenbury with you at White's the other day? Yes, I heard something said about him . . . about your taking his lands."

"That is only temporary. I felt the young fool needed a lesson. I had seen he was gambling much too impulsively, and there were many waiting to fleece such a young lamb. The estate is mine only if he fails to pay the debt in six months' time. He is now making the rounds of the bankers. One will be willing to loan him the sum if he can show a less brash nature in the next four months," Cavilon said reluctantly.

"But the land is yours till then? Would it not be a more forceful lesson if Tenbury were to see you occupy his manor?"

"*Mon ami*," Cavilon rose smiling, "*merci*." He paused in front of his desk. "But tell me, why was it you called?"

"Only to offer my felicitations," Tretain lied easily.

"You have found someone for the task you spoke of?" The comte cocked his head suspiciously.

"No," the earl laughed, "but you would be of little use in your present state. Be off to Ashford. I wish you the best of luck in your endeavour there." Tretain reached out and shook his friend's hand.

"*Merci*, and my greetings and apologies to Juliane

for not calling to bid her farewell in person. Send word if the situation with the other matter becomes desperate. Perhaps Martin shall have to make one last journey."

"Your services will be missed," Tretain told him seriously. "But then, we have learned never to depend on any one individual. *Bonne chance*," he added and took his leave.

Cavilon returned to his chair and sat deep in thought for several minutes, then rose and summoned Leveque. "We shall journey to Ashford in Kent in the morn," he told the valet. "I have acquired some property I wish to inspect. Prepare for a lengthy stay."

Putting the letter on her bureau after reading it a second time, Elizabeth continued to gaze at it, shaking her head. Ten days back at Ashly, back in the routine of running her uncle's household and seeing to the prodigious task of civilizing Tom and Barney, had helped to push thoughts of Cavilon back, if not entirely from her mind. Now this strange letter from Lady Tretain forced it all to the fore.

Surely my short note telling Lady Juliane that I was leaving London and could not call upon her could not have prompted this? she wondered. Had Cavilon himself prompted it? No, she thought, pacing to the oriel window of her bedroom. Even a man such as the comte did not reveal such things about himself as Lady Juliane had written of. *How strange to think of Cavilon as a man passionately in love with anyone*, Elizabeth mused, thinking of the letter's contents. *And how very sad that he was betrayed.* She recalled his words about ardour being tiresome, and deep pity for him arose. "He must have been terribly hurt . . ." She gasped. "Even as I was by Father's death." This sudden realization of the root cause of all her anger and hatred shocked her. "I turned against all things French," she murmured aloud, "and Cavilon . . . Why his overly foppish dress and mannerisms could all have been caused by a violent reaction to this woman's having played falsely with him."

And you, too, rejected him, came the sobering thought. *You rejected him harshly and without good cause or genteel manners.* Perturbed, Elizabeth hurried from her room and down the stairs. At the foot of them she encountered Niles. "I am going for a walk but shall return in time for tea," she told him.

"Should I call Spense to go with you, miss?"

"I am not in London now, Niles. Lady Waddington cannot object to my walking in my uncle's woods," she returned sharply.

"As you say, miss," the butler said impassively, walking before her and opening the doors.

Now, why did you have to snap at him? Elizabeth mentally rebuked herself as she strode down the gravel drive, then turned south to go into the woods beyond the rambling manor house. Entering the woods, her steps were slowed by brambles and broken limbs. Her thoughts became calmer. *Why should you be so upset?* she asked herself. *Cavilon is in London, and you are here. You never made any commitment to the man. In fact, you were tactlessly brutal about your feelings towards him. Lady Juliane must have misunderstood the reason for my returning here. Her letter changes nothing.*

But would it have, her conscience questioned, *if you had known what she has written before your last encounter with the comte?*

Shaking herself, Elizabeth forced the question aside and stamped forward, trying to find relief in physical exertion. Her thoughts left Cavilon and moved towards her father, until they strangely mingled. A deep sorrow filled her. Suddenly she felt very tired. Looking about, she saw that she had come much deeper into the woods than she had meant, but she breathed a sigh of thanksgiving for the privacy this gave her. Slowly Elizabeth sat beneath the shade of the large beech trees. Tears welled in her eyes. *Nothing is right anymore,* she thought. *My steady, safe world has gone awry, and there is nothing I can do to set it right.* Her head hung, huge tear drops fell onto her skirt; for the first time in many years she cried freely, sobbing deeply. Sometime later the tears had slowed, but the ache held stubbornly fast. She attempted to dry her eyes with the edge of her skirt.

"La, Miss Jeffries, must you be so thorough in everything you do?" sounded a nasal drawl at her side.

The unexpected voice caused her to start violently. "Cavilon," she gasped, disbelieving the sight in puce satin and lace before her.

"It is terribly un-English to carry on so." The comte tossed his second kerchief to her lap. "But seeing how you have done a"—he tapped his cheek reflectively—"I believe it is called 'a bloody good job of it,' I daresay it can be disregarded as unpatriotic."

For a moment anger surged through Elizabeth; then, studying Cavilon's ridiculous pose and considering his even more absurd words, she burst into laughter.

A lace kerchief fluttered to Cavilon's lips, concealing his smile of relief.

Elizabeth held her hand out, then withdrew it. "I forgot. You mustn't soil your gloves," she teased, still laughing.

"But if they are removed, then they cannot be soiled," Cavilon said lightly, deftly removing the white gloves and tossing them to the ground. With an elaborate bow, he offered his hand to assist her up.

The sudden seriousness in his features dispelled the foppishness, but the look was gone in an instance. An awkward silence descended as Elizabeth stood, conscious only of the firm gentleness of his hold.

"My lord." She finally removed her hand. "How do you come to be here? I would not have thought our English countryside would be attractive to you."

"La, Miss Jeffries, even I tire of . . . society. I . . . my dear, what are you doing?" Cavilon feigned shock.

"There is no reason to waste a perfectly good pair of gloves," she told him, picking his off the ground. Handing them to the comte, she said, "And now, will you tell me why you are here? Are you a guest of Lord Tenbury?"

"I doubt that he would think so. I won his estate in a game of hazard," Cavilon noted carefully.

"It certainly was a hazardous game for Lord Tenbury," Elizabeth said with lightly concealed surprise.

"A lesson to the unwise," the comte quipped, then added, "I am most pleased to see you somewhat restored to your usual mien, Miss Jeffries. Was the matter serious?"

"My lord, we all know you are never serious," she answered lightly.

"La, you have understood me perfectly. Can you not see how well we would deal together?"

"Uncle Henry would not agree, but then he does not value his toilet as highly as you do yours. Nor is his as . . . striking as yours." She paused, a finger on her chin, and surveyed him from peruke to shoes.

"Dare I hope, Miss Jeffries, that you are not of your uncle's thinking?" he asked, half serious, half teasing.

"Oh, I assure you, my lord, I think your dress as memorable as Uncle Henry does," she quipped.

"And how do Tom and his four-footed friend fare?" Cavilon retreated.

"Why, you remember his name!" Elizabeth was surprised. "Actually, once we found Aunt Waddie's, Lady Waddington," she explained, the inflection of her voice warning Cavilon not to utter the quip on the tip of his tongue, "once we found her vinaigrette and explained that Barney was not a lion, all went fairly well. I am currently trying to teach Tom how to be a page but," she shrugged hopelessly, "I doubt I have the patience for such work. The experience has almost destroyed my hopes of being a governess." She forced a smile. "But it will soon go better."

"Have you thought Tom might be better suited to being a groom, having worked with animals, that is?" the comte suggested with a yawn.

Elizabeth frowned deeply at him, then shook her head, realizing that he was simply baiting her with his attitude. "I shall consider that," she finally said, smiling begrudgingly. "Now I must go . . . before Barney is sent in search of me. Naturally the distance to Ashly is too far for you to even consider walking," she noted dryly.

"*Naturellement*," Cavilon agreed with a wry smile. "But I shall see you again . . . *ma petite*."

Shaking her head, Elizabeth laughed gently. "Perhaps," she spoke softly. Stepping away from him briskly, she retraced her steps. A distance away she paused briefly and glanced back to find Cavilon still gazing after her. Upon impulse she waved at him, but turned before he could respond. *If nothing else is in his behalf*, she thought, *he can make me laugh*.

Barney's loud barking told Elizabeth that she was nearing Ashly. At the edge of the wood she halted and watched a rider mount and ride away. When he was out of sight, she dashed forward, thinking he might have brought word from her brother.

Hearing the front doors slam, Lady Waddington paused at midstair.

"Was that a message from Morton?" Elizabeth asked, hurrying to her.

Regret crossed her aunt's features. "No, my dear. The rider brought an invitation. The Chatworths are having a day party on Tuesday next. From the note

Mrs. Chatworth enclosed, I gather that it is to be an elite gathering. I am so happy we were able to do some shopping before Henry rushed us home. I do hope he returns in time to escort us."

"Yes," murmured Elizabeth, wondering if the comte would be at the gathering.

Chapter XIII

Looking from her window the morn after the invitation was received, Elizabeth saw a rider approaching Ashly and recognized the younger Miss Chatworth. A smile came to her face, as she looked forward to the coze.

Suzanne Chatworth, although five years younger, was a close friend of Elizabeth's, the two having enjoyed trips to the lending library in Ashford, as well as long walks and other country pursuits permitted to ladies of genteel upbringing, ever since the younger was released from the schoolroom. Suzanne's lighter, more effusive nature effectively balanced Elizabeth's more serious inclinations, and the two took great pleasure in their visits.

This morn Suzanne's colour was more heightened than usual as she flowed into the small salon where the two oft met. She pursed her lips tightly, taking a seat opposite her friend, and primly removed her gloves.

"You shall burst," Elizabeth told her dryly, "if you keep the news inside a moment longer. I know that look."

Suzanne scooted to the edge of her seat, but she eased back as Lady Waddington came into the salon. She fielded all of Lady Waddington's queries about the day party with effusive babble. Her girlish chatter brought Lady Madeline to a standstill, and she excused herself.

"I thought Lady Waddie would never leave," burst from the young woman the moment the door closed. She jumped up eagerly and plopped down beside Elizabeth on the sofa. "My mother made me promise on my honour not to tell Lady Waddie who is coming to our day party," Suzanne trilled the word, "but that does not include you. It will be the most glamorous party we have ever had." She clapped her hands in delight. "You must wear your very best gown, for there are to be two eligibles present." Suzanne paused and wrinkled her nose at Elizabeth's lack of interest. "There will be Lord Fromby, who is visiting with the Newcombs . . . and . . . the Comte de Cavilon. Father says he is quite plump in the pocket and an excellent catch. Do you think I might stand a chance of snaring him?" She patted a golden curl into place.

"Why . . . why I would not think you would want to," Elizabeth stuttered. "I mean, I thought there was a gentleman who had captured your heart two years past. It does not matter to me if you must try for the comte, but you must realize he is vastly different from the gentlemen we are accustomed to. Why, he does not hunt or ride and goes about in powdered peruke and even wears facial powder and rouge. What *did* become of that young man you have always refused to name?" Elizabeth asked, apparently having developed a sudden interest in her friend's past love.

With a wave of her hand Suzanne dismissed the question. "Is the comte quite old then?" she asked. "Perhaps I might wed him and become a wealthy widow."

"Suzanne!" Elizabeth looked askance at her friend. "How can you say such words? The Comte de Cavilon is . . . Well, he is neither young nor old, but not young enough to make you a suitable husband or old enough to make you soon a widow. But why ask me about him?" she ended exasperatedly, upset as much by the other's interest as by her voiced intent.

"Because," Suzanne leaned close, "Lady Waddie called on Mother shortly after you returned, and you should have heard what she said about the comte. Most unfit for maidenly ears," she tisked.

"Then why did you listen?" Elizabeth's annoyance tinged her words.

"It was so fascinating. The Comte de Cavilon offered for someone known to Lady Waddie. A shame she did not say who." Suzanne sighed, watching Elizabeth closely. "But she did tell Mother that he rescued you both from a terrible carriage accident while you were in London, so I knew you had seen him. Is he ghastly handsome?"

"No. Yes . . . I mean , no. And the accident was a minor happening." Miss Jeffries felt her cheeks warm.

"Why Elizabeth, are you angry at me?" Suzanne paused.

"Of course not," she returned contritely.

"Then tell me about the Comte de Cavilon. Perhaps

137

he will save me from being put on the shelf as you have been." She arched an eyebrow.

"I doubt you will find the comte that appealing," Elizabeth said curtly.

"Oh, we shall see," the other said with a coy smile.

Watching the coquettish pose, Elizabeth began to wonder what her friend was about. She surely did not mean to try for Cavilon?

"You are interested in the comte?" Suzanne questioned.

"Of course not." Elizabeth forced a laugh.

"I am so happy to hear that," the young woman said, rising. "Now I must go. There is so much to be done." She brushed the other's cheek with a kiss. "No need to see me out. Remember, wear your most attractive gown. We can, perhaps, interest Lord Fromby in you," Suzanne prattled, and fluttered from the salon.

Her friend's visit prompted Elizabeth to return to her room and examine her suddenly meagre wardrobe. The most stylish of her gowns was the icy green muslin she had worn to the Tretains' ball. At odds with her usual practical nature, she dismissed it as an impossibility. "I don't know what to wear Tuesday for the Chatworths' party," she told Spense, who had entered with some daygowns she had just finished ironing.

"Why, the green muslin, miss," the abigail answered, taken aback by this sudden interest in gowns.

"No, I cannot wear it. If only the other gowns we ordered while in London had been delivered. The deep blue would have been perfect. It was a soft muslin with the new high waistline," she told an astounded Spense, "trimmed at the sleeve, hem, and neckline with a deeper blue piping and white lace. . . . Yes?" A knock turned Elizabeth to the door.

"Sir Henry has returned," Niles told her. "He wishes to see you at once."

"Oh, he will have news of Tom," she said excitedly. "Leave things as they are, we shall continue when I return."

Sir Henry greeted his niece cordially. "Happy to see you looking so fit. Hoped you wouldn't have any nonsense like pining away for that Cavilon. Rumours abounding in London about the man. Some say he won Tenbury's lands in a game of hazard. They are all wondering why he has disappeared without a word." Sir Henry shook his head. "Knew my decision was for the best." He patted her clumsily on the shoulder. "Your trip to London was not a total loss, however," he said, smiling brightly. "I have brought with me the gowns you and Madeline ordered. Thought you might enjoy having them."

"Oh, thank you, Uncle Henry," she said, filled with relief. "But what of Tom?"

A subtle hardening of the lines across his features portended ill. "The lad will have to return to London."

"But why?"

"He ran away from his master three months past and must be returned," he told her firmly.

"Tom said he was an orphan," Elizabeth protested.

"That is true enough, but he was bound to a Mr.

Bickle before his father died and must serve his term. The law is not to be mocked."

"But there must have been some reason for him to run away. What work did this man have him do?"

"Honest work . . . that of a chimney sweep."

"Don't you see, Uncle? Tom is getting much too large for that kind of work. You yourself have told me of the abuses, how some masters light fires beneath the boys' feet to force them up the chimneys. You cannot mean to send Tom back," she pleaded.

"I am satisfied that Mr. Bickle is a fair man. He will not use the lad in the chimneys but for running errands. The matter is no longer in my hands. Mr. Bickle came with me and is taking Tom back in the morn. This will be for the best. We cannot have you taking in every ragamuffin you see. Now go and try on the gowns. That will raise your spirits," Sir Henry told her gruffly, his conscience beginning to trouble him.

"Has Tom been told? Then I will do so," Elizabeth said, hurrying from the room. Going outdoors, she heard Barney's angry barks coming from the stable. When she entered, she saw a sparse man towering threateningly over Tom with only Barney preventing him from thrashing the boy soundly. Rushing forward, she grabbed the dog by the collar. "Quiet, Barney. Quiet, now," she commanded and was amazed when he obeyed.

"The lad be mine," the man said belligerently.

"But not yours to abuse. He will go with you in the morn," she retorted.

"Ye'll not be taking that beast with ye," Bickle swore, looking past her at the lad. His eyes went back to Elizabeth and wavered. He turned and stomped out of the stable.

"Ye ain't lettin' him take me?" Tears welled in Tom's eyes. "Ye can't let me go. Ye don't know what he'll do ta me."

"I know," Elizabeth put her free arm about the boy's shaking shoulders, "but you must go with him. It will only be for a short time, though. I promise."

Huge, tear-filled eyes were raised to hers. "Ye promise?"

"Yes," she swore, "and I'll take care of Barney till you return."

"God bless ye, miss." The lad pressed her hand gratefully. "I believe ye'll do it."

The lad's trust shook Elizabeth. What if she were not able to do as she had promised?

Returning to the house, she hurried to her room. The abigail had removed the blue gown from its box and laid it across the bed. A glance at it sent Elizabeth to her writing desk. "You may go, Spense." She motioned for the abigail to leave. "I will call you when I need you. Seated before the desk, Elizabeth drew out paper and dipped her pen. Did she dare ask this of Cavilon? *I have to, there is no one else,* she thought, and hurriedly wrote.

Early next morn Elizabeth stole from the house and searched for Tom, finding him in the stables. Giving the lad the few coins she had, she instructed him to do as his master commanded and remain out of trouble until his bond was purchased. This done, she accepted the piece of rope he had tied to Barney's collar.

"Best keep him close ta ye, miss," Tom instructed. "Yer the only one 'sides me he pays a mind to. And he may try 'n follow me. Old man Bickle'll harm him if he 'as the chance," he ended with a frown.

"Don't worry. I'll see to his care. Now do as I told you."

"Aye, miss."

Farewells done, Elizabeth tugged at Barney's collar and managed to get him to follow. Halfway to the house the huge dog suddenly halted and looked back to the stables with a soft whine. Tom came running and hugged the large animal tightly.

"Listen, Barney," he commanded through his tears, "ye go with miss here. Guard her till I get back. Get now." He rose and scuffed his foot at the dog.

Reluctantly Barney yielded to Elizabeth's urgings and followed. She did not halt till she had him safely in her room. "I must go down for breakfast now. When I return, we shall go for a nice long walk," she told the dog, patting his woolly head. With a prayer that the beast would not do too much damage, she left him.

Returning a half hour later, breakfast having been bolted down, she was overwhelmingly relieved to find Barney lying quietly by the fireplace. "Good boy," she congratulated him. "Now for our walk."

Heaven knows the Comte de Cavilon will not be about at this early hour, she thought as they made their way down the stairs, *but I wish no delay. I shall await him . . . if he comes at all.*

Niles opened the door for the pair without showing a hint of his surprise, murmuring only when he closed the door, "Heaven perserve us."

Barney strained towards the stables, but he followed Elizabeth's tugs and was soon trotting quite willingly at her side when they reached the woods. Arriving at the place she had given for their meeting, she gasped. Cavilon awaited her.

"My lord, 'tis so early," Elizabeth stammered uncertainly.

"Your note, *ma petite*, said the matter was most urgent. I knew you would come early, and it would have been most ungentlemanly to have kept you waiting. Knowing your thoroughness, I concluded the hour would be sunrise. You disappoint me." The comte sauntered forward slowly, halting but a step from her.

"You can't mean you . . . You were not . . ." Elizabeth stuttered, then read the tease in his eyes and sighed with relief.

"Did you feel in danger that you must bring this?" Cavilon waved languidly at Barney.

"Oh, no." She blushed at his implication. "He is the reason I wrote. Well, not really. It is his master," she stumbled over her words, disconcerted by his nearness. "Tom is being sent back to London," she hurried on. "He ran away from his master, a cruel chimney-sweep master, and I fear the man will . . . I fear for Tom." She met his gaze.

"And you wish me to do something about this?" Cavilon took hold of her free hand.

143

"Couldn't you . . . Couldn't you pay Mr. Bickle to release Tom?" Elizabeth asked breathlessly, feeling that his deep stare was looking into her very soul.

"And what would I be given for doing this?" he asked, then immediately placed a finger on her lips. "We shall speak of that another time. Do not fear. The lad shall be saved." The comte had leaned forward as he spoke. His words ended, his lips softly claimed hers. "It shall be done for you, *ma chère petite*." He stepped back and bowed with a flourish.

Barney tugged at the rope, forcing Elizabeth to look to him. When she turned back, Cavilon was gone. A mist of confusion swirled through her. Tom was saved, but what of herself?

Chapter XIV

The afternoon of the Chatworths' festivities proved to be splendidly un-English. Warm sunshine and a soft breeze dispelled the mist and any hint of clouds long before the guests arrived.

Mrs. Chatworth beamed proudly as she watched the assembled party walking before her in the large formal garden, which was her pride. The low, neatly trimmed hedges, planted in geometric patterns, gave mute testimony to the neatness of the English spirit, while their gay, flowering centers bespoke the lustiness of the English nature. Never had her gardens been so flourishing or her guests so elegant, she thought, her eyes resting upon the Comte de Cavilon and her daughter Suzanne.

Seeing that the gentlemen were becoming restless, Mrs. Chatworth directed the party to the broad green lawns beyond the gardens. Tables and chairs had been arranged in the shade of huge oaks, and a plentiful supply of food and drink awaited.

The group moved slowly, separating. The younger members took to the game of bowls which had been set up in one area, or to a game similar to croquet in another. The older gentlemen happily sat down to a game of whist, while the ladies ensured proper chaperoning of the young people.

Elizabeth's trepidation at facing Cavilon after their encounter in the woods was slowly dispelled, for he was equally attentive to all the ladies. She was further relieved to find her uncle willing to abide the comte's presence. Evading Lord Fromby's grimly determined pursuit, she saw Suzanne's frequent smile and knew who was responsible for his unwanted attention. There being no polite way of eluding the man, Elizabeth endeavoured to make the best of the day and consented to a game of croquet while trying to observe Cavilon and Suzanne without appearing obvious. She did not know whether to be chagrined or relieved that he had dropped his intimate manner and was coolly polite to her. Seeing Suzanne lay a hand on Cavilon's arm and laugh at some comment he made, she tapped her ball without checking the direction.

"Miss Jeffries," Lord Fromby's irksome voice called her to task. "Where are you going? The hoop is in this direction. You shall never progress if you do not pay attention," he complained. "I prefer a close game."

"I am sorry, my lord. I shall try to do better," Elizabeth said sweetly as she walked to her ball. Determindedly making up the lost distance, she soon found her ball near Fromby's. Snapping the mallet sharply to her ball, she sent it roqueting against Fromby's. "Is that better, my lord?" she asked, her mallet still poised above her head.

"Yes, yes," Fromby grumbled, wondering why he

had ever let Miss Chatworth wheedle him into promising to flatter Miss Jeffries. He had disliked attending the day party, his distaste for such pleasures having long since ruled out simple country affairs, and now sought relief for his boredom. Glancing about, his eye lit upon the Comte de Cavilon. "I say, Miss Jeffries, why do we not put our mallets up and watch those playing bowls. My lord Cavilon's style should be excessively entertaining."

His tone caused her to frown, but she permitted him to lead her to Mrs. Chatworth, who was watching the game with interest.

"Your daughter is excessively pretty," Fromby noted archly, admiring Suzanne's neat waist and flushed cheeks. "What a shame," he mused.

"Yes, my lord?" their hostess turned questioningly to him.

"It is only that your daughter appears partial to my lord Cavilon"—Fromby raised his voice slightly—"and we all know that will lead to naught. The comte, you know, has never shown interest in any but his own petticoats."

Mrs. Chatworth and the women near Fromby gasped at his words; Elizabeth looked to Cavilon and was disappointed to see him pointedly ignoring the words.

"Surely you would like some refreshment, my lord," Lady Chatworth suggested, trying to draw the man towards the tables.

"We must even be amazed his lordship consented to such a demanding form of entertainment," Fromby continued, refusing to move. "One wonders if . . ."

147

"My lord Fromby," Elizabeth interrupted him, her colour high not only because of her anger at his words but also for the comte's lack of care for them. "Your manners are wanting."

Visions of her day party becoming a shambles spurred Mrs. Chatworth into action. "Elizabeth, I just remembered that Lady Madeline asked for a glass of lemonade. Would you please fetch it for her? And Lord Fromby, you were speaking . . ."

He waved her words aside. "Miss Jeffries, do I understand that you wish to defend my lord Cavilon?" He turned to those standing about. "I suppose it is only proper he be defended by a female," Fromby sneered. "It is just as proper if you were to champion that notorious brigand Martin," he continued sarcastically. "But perhaps that cause would be more worthwhile, for the man may be a high-handed rogue and a blackguard, but at least he is a man."

"If you speak so highly of him, my lord, I could not but admire him," Elizabeth returned hotly, her cheeks burning beneath the embarrassed glances of those about them.

Fromby was not to be put aside. "If you had encountered him as I have, you would not be speaking so snappily." He raised his head haughtily. "While I was defending the shores of our dear homeland, having successfully captured a vessel laden with contraband, he and his men attacked my ship. Why, the man has only one name," he sneered. "I imagine his mother could not pick out the father," Fromby snorted, enjoying his crude jest. "This bastard had the audacity to attack us and threw everyone into the sea. Then he stole away; but I recovered all," his lordship finished smugly.

"La, Fromby, you are brave, *n'est-ce pas?*" Cavilon eyed the man disdainfully. "To think I was told that only you were thrown overboard and that your men were so glad to be rid of you that they assisted this Martin. But then," he fluttered his lace, "one should never listen to a gabblemonger . . . should one?"

His lordship failed to catch the comte's point. "They shall not speak so when the rogue is captured. Just barely two months past this was almost achieved. Landing on the Dover coast, I pursued him to Folkestone, and it was only the soldiers' ineptness that let him slip through my grasp. No doubt he was aided by someone of your persuasion." He turned condemningly to Elizabeth.

The name of Folkestone and the time mentioned brought a vivid memory to her. "What does this man look like?" she asked weakly.

"He is a dark devil, a tall man. But for all his size," Fromby snorted, "he has not dared show himself since that night. If they had allowed me to command, he would not now be free," he bragged. "Come, Mrs. Chatworth." His lordship offered his arm to her. "I believe I would like a glass of sherry."

"Are you quite all right?" Suzanne asked, joining Elizabeth as the others walked away. "You look as if a spirit had appeared before you." She attempted to joke lightly, but failed.

"Do you remember," Elizabeth said lowly, "in March, the man who forced his way into my coach? It must have been this Martin."

"Then you must be fortunate indeed, if Lord Fromby's words are to be believed," Cavilon's nasal drawl announced. "But I cannot wonder that this Monsieur Martin is a very dauntless fellow to have dared his lordship and *you* in one eve," he teased.

Some colour returned as she searched the comte's features, trying to understand his behaviour.

"I believe you mentioned a stream, Miss Chatworth. Could we not seek out its beauty?" Cavilon suggested, his eyes flicking to Fromby and back.

"Oh, yes. I am certain you will find it delightful," Suzanne agreed readily. "Come with us, Elizabeth."

"I . . . I do not—"

"Come. Father has had some of his rods placed near the stream and you know you love to fish," the younger woman prompted.

"Come, Miss Jeffries. You must demonstrate this for me." Cavilon stepped forward and offered his arm. "Mayhaps you could ask Lady Waddington to join us," he suggested to Suzanne.

"An excellent idea." She smiled broadly. "You two go on, and we shall come at once."

"But Lady Madeline detests coming near water," Elizabeth objected.

"Then I shall ask Sir Henry or Father." Suzanne was not to be stayed.

Cavilon nodded gravely and Elizabeth took his arm, telling him the direction of the stream as they walked along. After a brief silence the comte halted. "May I always be so ably defended," he spoke quietly. "I thank you."

Blushing, Elizabeth dropped her eyes.

"I notice that you do not have your guardian with you today," the comte began, walking forward slowly again.

"Guardian?" she questioned. "Oh, Barney." She laughed, forcing her thoughts to the present. "He did follow our coach, but we turned back and Uncle had him tied with a stout rope. What of Tom?" Her eyes went to him eagerly.

"The matter should be settled. The lad may be on his way back even now," Cavilon told her as they halted before the stream. He studied her closely for a moment. "This man, Martin. Are you certain it was he whom you encountered?"

"It matters not," she said simply.

"Then he did you no harm?"

"No. He was almost . . . gallant," Elizabeth answered softly, the inflection of her voice revealing much. Giving herself a shake, she eyed the comte critically. "Why did you let Lord Fromby speak so of you?"

"What would you have me do? Challenge him? You forget your laws now frown on affairs of honour," the comte told her. "Nor do I think our hostess would have approved. But," he looked away from her gaze, "we are at the stream. Let us see if you can ply the rod as Miss Chatworth says. I myself do not care for the sport."

"A fish is hardly a dangerous adversary, my lord," Elizabeth told him caustically. Seeing the rods to one side, she picked one up and walked a short distance downstream. After a few adjustments, she baited the hook and began casting with precision.

"Mayhaps I have misjudged the sport," the comte said, following her. "It does not appear difficult."

"There is no one preventing you from trying your hand," she observed coldly.

"But I must be shown how it is done," he answered, stepping very close. "If I could but put my hand upon yours as you throw it . . ."

"Cast, my lord. One does not throw a line, but 'casts' it." Elizabeth frowned more deeply, realizing that he was again teasing. Her breath was taken away as one of his hands closed firmly over hers on the pole. The other went about her waist.

"My lord—"

"Are you not going to cast?" he asked innocently, looking deep into her upraised eyes.

A deep growl caused the comte to let loose his hold and turn protectively. He was met with the full force of Barney as the dog leaped at him. Lying spread-eagled on the ground, the dog's paws on his chest, Cavilon grinned wryly. "La, Miss Jeffries, I do believe the rope was not stout enough. I do hope the beast is not *dangereux*?"

Barney responded by lapping at Cavilon's face, and Elizabeth burst into laughter. She laid down her pole and tugged at the dog's collar.

"I do think he has taken a liking to you, my lord," she managed between peals of laughter. "Now we are even," she told him as Barney finally consented to move and the comte was able to rise.

"But where is your coach to rescue me?" Cavilon motioned to his paw-printed pantaloons and jacket.

"Oh, I am sorry." Instant regret came to Elizabeth's features.

"It matters not," he assured her, brushing at the worst marks. "If it brought a smile to your lips, it cannot be but good. I regret only that it shall force me to depart."

"If only you could go without Lord Fromby seeing . . ."

"His lordship's words cannot harm me, *ma petite*. Only a man who has reason to be can be shamed." Cavilon took her hand and kissed it.

"Why, my lord," Suzanne's voice intruded, "what has happened? Isn't that Barney?" she asked, seeing the dog at her friend's side.

"It is," Elizabeth answered above Barney's greeting.

"And I must take my leave," the comte bowed. "My appearance, I fear, has suffered somewhat from our meeting."

Barney barked once more, then hung his head contritely.

"What's this?" Sir Henry asked, joining the group. "Lud, Cavilon, what's happened to you? Thought that beast was tied, Elizabeth," he blustered. "My apologies, Cavilon."

A languid wave of the comte's hand answered him. "No need, sir."

"What a bloody beast of a brute you have there," Lord Fromby told Elizabeth as he sauntered up to them. "What happened, Cavilon? Trip on your lace?"

A low growl came from Barney.

"Is the beast safe?" Fromby stepped back.

"Your animal has excellent taste, Miss Jeffries," Cavilon told her, speaking loud enough for Fromby to hear.

"What do you mean?" His lordship stepped towards the comte. "No popinjay of a dandy will insult me."

"Insult you, my lord? I shudder at the thought." Cavilon's kerchief fluttered to the ground. He stepped backward with feigned fright. "La, me," he tisked, reaching to retrieve it.

What happened next was not clear to anyone. Cavilon appeared to stumble and lurched forward, grabbing hold of Fromby's jacket to right himself. The two men tripped in a circular movement, and in the end Fromby was pitched into the stream while the comte mysteriously remained upright on the bank.

Barney broke from Elizabeth's hold and went after Fromby, yapping excitedly.

After Elizabeth managed to persuade the dog to return to her, Fromby, soaking wet and thoroughly outraged, climbed from the stream.

"My lord," Cavilon noted quietly as the enraged man moved slowly towards him, "it was a mere accident. I slipped upon my lace."

Suzanne and Elizabeth could no longer control themselves and burst into laughter. Even Sir Henry yielded to the ludicrous scene.

Giving each a fierce scowl, Fromby stalked away angrily.

Lord Cavilon permitted himself a weary smile.

"Never knew lace could be so dangerous." Sir Henry clapped him on the back. "Mayhaps I erred in my judgment. Bloody well done," he applauded.

"Oh, I insist it was an accident," the comte told him.

"As you say," Sir Henry agreed, eyeing him sternly. "There are some questions and answers we should discuss." He motioned for Cavilon to follow him.

The comte bowed elaborately to the two young women, excusing himself.

"I have never seen anyone like his lordship," Suzanne told Elizabeth with an admiring sigh as they walked back to the lawns. "Do you think I shall be able to take his interest?"

"I don't know," Elizabeth answered vaguely, wondering just what she herself thought of Cavilon.

Chapter XV

Cavilon returned home from the Chatworth party early in the eve. He immediately retired to his chambers on the ground floor of Tenbury's manor house and sent for Leveque.

"I am quite fatigued from the activities of the day," he told the valet as he disrobed. "I wish to sleep late into the day on the morrow. See that I am not disturbed for any reason. I shall call you when I need you." The comte waved dismissal.

"Yes, my lord," Leveque murmured, assisting his master into his dressing gown. "Good eve, my lord."

Cavilon sat before the fireplace, contemplating the day's happenings. When full darkness had fallen, he stepped quietly to the door and locked it. The drapes were drawn over the windows. Pulling his powdered peruke from his head, he began the transformation. When it was complete, the comte stood before his mirror once again as the tall, dark Martin. But he did not feel the freedom he had expected. Somehow he was not just a prisoner of Cavilon but of Martin also.

Extinguishing the lamps, he slipped from the room, using one of its windows. It took little skill to extract a mount from the stables, and in moments he was riding through the woods connecting the Tenbury and Jeffries properties.

Ashly came into view, and he drew his mount to a halt. The temptation to enter the house and visit Elizabeth was strong, but he quelled it, realizing he knew nothing of the house's arrangement and had no wish to encounter Barney. With regret he prodded the steed on, heading towards Folkestone, its harbour and its sailors, who he hoped would be able to give him the information he wished concerning the Chatworths' obnoxious guest.

Lord Fromby's presence at the day party, an affair vastly out of the man's general line, had been enough to rouse Cavilon's suspicions. Fromby had appeared on the London scene only three years past and had dealt with the more raffish set of the *ton*. The fact that he was sporadically short of funds was well known by all but had not struck the comte as particulary notable until the comment made today about having regained his ship. The sloop had, Cavilon knew, been pirated in the first place, and it seemed curious that it should have been in Fromby's possession in February. That the man had regained it was very telling, and the comte believed that there was more to dislike in his lordship than his insulting manners. His suspicions, Cavilon hoped, would be satisfied this night. Then action would be taken.

Cavilon began to relax as he rode, the freedom of movement a relief from the tedium of his other pose. A smile lightened his dark looks as he thought of Sir Henry's questions. The old man was keen on a scent that he could not risk having him follow. It would be embarrassing, the comte thought, to be undone in the end by an unsuspecting magistrate. Experience had taught him, however, that the more unlikely an event the more possible it became. His own foolishness had not helped him. It had been unwise to tumble Fromby, but vastly enjoyable. The thought brought a frown to his lips. Never since his youth had he let the desire to please a woman guide him; it was not a good sign that he was bending Cavilon to please Elizabeth, for he could not be certain it was not his wealth that drew her.

Was her sudden softening towards him due to it, or because of what he had done for the lad, Tom? Did he dare hope it was himself who attracted her? Then he recalled the inflection of her voice when she had spoken, ever so briefly, of Martin. He had heard that tone in a woman's voice many times, oft using the feeling it bespoke to his own advantage. As long as she could be drawn to the more attractive of his personalities, he was forced to doubt her. If given a choice now, Martin pondered, which would she choose?

Waking in the morn from a fitful sleep, Elizabeth turned over to find Barney sitting at her bedside, staring at her with large, soulful eyes. "You," she said accusingly, then reached out and patted the shaggy head. "It was Lord Fromby you should have given a tumble to yesterday," she told him, sitting up in bed. "I wonder what would have happened had you not come when you did? Well, it matters not what the

Comte de Cavilon meant to do, but what you did do. We must teach you better manners." Elizabeth swung her feet out of bed, and the large dog ran to the door. "I suppose Niles is wondering where you are," she said, following him. "Don't drag the poor footman quite as far afield this morn," she called after him as he pranced down the corridor. "I shall be glad when Tom returns." She spoke to herself, dressing. "I wonder how soon that shall be?" Musing over this brought to mind her brother, whom Tom had reminded her of in many ways. It had been too long since they had heard from him. Perhaps her uncle could learn how he was faring. Her toilet complete, she went down to breakfast.

Sir Henry entered a few moments later, a letter in his hand and a large smile on his face. "This has just come," he said, waving the missive at her. "I am certain it is from Morton."

"I was just thinking of him this morn," she said eagerly. "Do open it. What of the messenger?"

"The letter was brought to the door by a local lad. He said someone had stopped him and paid him to bring it to me. He had never seen the man before. Nothing to be learned there. Those who ply between the shores these days are not eager to be known," he answered as he broke the letter's seal.

"What does it say? Is he well?" Elizabeth asked, watching her uncle read. "What is it?" she questioned, seeing the worry flicker across his face.

"The boy sends his love," Sir Henry answered, "and says that they have been treating him much the same as when he last wrote. The money I sent him arrived."

He read further. "And he was able to get better food for a time." There was another pause as he reread the next portion of the letter. "He has been moved to another prison. He says they were taken at night and it was raining. He has developed a cough."

"Then he is ill," Elizabeth gasped. "Has a doctor seen him?"

"It seems the money is all gone and medicines are very expensive, but he says he will probably be rid of it soon." Sir Henry laid the letter down. "You would think they would have at least told him where he is being held."

"When was the letter written, Uncle Henry?"

"Written?" He looked at the top of the page. "The date has been smeared. Heaven knows how many hands this has gone through in getting to us. It looks to be May . . . no, March," he told her.

"Why, that was almost three months past," she exclaimed. "I wonder if he is better now?"

"Little else we can do, my dear," her uncle noted matter-of-factly as he perused the letter once more. "Hrrummph, he says to give greetings to the Chatworths. Odd, I do believe he has mentioned them each time he has written. No matter." Sir Henry shrugged the triviality aside. "Do wish we could learn where he is. Makes getting funds to him devilishly more difficult, if not bloody well impossible. I wonder if Cavilon would have any ideas? He would be familiar with the land and all. Probably not. The man seems to take little note of anything important. Though at times . . ." His words trailed off.

"Yes, Uncle?" Elizabeth wondered what he meant.

"Nothing. We had better eat before the food grows cold. Oh, since the comte is now our neighbor, I have given him leave to call upon us. Yesterday he complained of country living being exceedingly dull, and I decided it would do little harm to be neighbourly. Likely he will not remain here long."

"Did he speak of returning to London?"

"Would you be sorry to see him go?" He cocked his head at her.

"There is no reason for me to be. My mind has not been altered. I merely find him . . . amusing. Have you changed your thoughts of him?" she questioned, taking a biscuit from the platter Niles had set before them.

"No, and you'll do wise to see he does no more than amuse you. There is something strange about Cavilon, something I cannot quite determine. It has been nagging at me. For now let us say I would rather the fox be in my lair than I in his." Sir Henry chuckled and refused to explain.

"Good afternoon, Lady Waddington, Miss Jeffries." The Comte de Cavilon bowed with a flourish. "I hope my arrival is not an inconvenience."

"Do join us, my lord," Lady Madeline greeted him cheerfully. "Would you care to partake of a cup of tea with us?"

"I have not yet accustomed myself to your English habit," he declined graciously. "Is Sir Henry at home?"

"There was some matter he had to take care of in Ashford," Lady Waddington answered. "It seems an unusual amount of contraband is arriving here, though how they know that, I do not understand. I do think he shall return soon," she told him. "Do be seated. Are you settled in at Tenbury?"

"I have done little more than look over the property since I arrived. I find it difficult to begin. To make a house one's home is a difficult task."

"Do you find our houses so very different from those in your own country?" Elizabeth asked.

"England is now my country," he returned softly.

"I did not mean otherwise," she met his gaze, "but surely you find things vastly dissimilar here. Do you have the comfort of hearing from your family still in France?"

"I fear not, Miss Jeffries. There is none of my family left, and what friends I had who did not escape died during the bloody days of the Terror. Why do you ask?"

"I simply realized that you never mention anyone from France or even seem to have much to do with other émigrés, but then, I am becoming too personal. My curiosity was prompted by something Uncle said this morn." She looked back to the stitching she had laid aside.

"A letter arrived this morn from Elizabeth's brother, Morton," Lady Waddington told Cavilon. "Sir Henry was thinking that perhaps you might be able to tell us what prison he could have been moved to."

Cavilon shook his head questioningly, his hand raised in a gesture of uncertainty.

"Morton spoke of being moved, and Uncle Henry thought you, having lived in France since your birth, would be familiar with the prisons that exist and know the most logical choice. I find it difficult to understand why Morton does not know where he is being held," Elizabeth ended with a frown.

"That is not so difficult," Cavilon explained. "The prisoners are moved only at night, and the name of their new home is never spoken. It discourages escape attempts. I do hope your brother is faring well."

"He has been, but in this letter he mentions a cough taking hold."

You know how dangerous that can be," Lady Waddington sighed.

"What does trouble me," Elizabeth added, "is that the letter was written in March. So much could have happened to him since then."

"It is such a worry," Lady Madeline sighed once again. "Henry is so concerned."

And with reason, Cavilon thought, knowing the pitiful conditions most prisoners of war were forced to endure. "I have heard from London," he said, deciding that a different topic might prove more cheerful.

"Elizabeth, the Comte de Cavilon has news of the lad you brought with us," Lady Waddington intruded into her niece's thoughts.

"I am sorry, my lord." She smiled faintly. "You mentioned London?"

"Tom will be returning to Ashford in a few days, perhaps a week," Cavilon told her. "My agent has purchased his bond and has taken the boy into his home. There are a few matters of business he must attend to, and then he shall bring the lad to me."

"Oh, that is good news, I do not know how to thank

you," Elizabeth exclaimed. "Shall you take him into your household?"

"I rather thought he might prefer to be with you . . . if that is acceptable to Sir Henry. That is what I wished to see him about," Cavilon answered. "Does that displease you?" he asked as dismay came to her eyes.

"No, it is as I wish," Elizabeth answered. "I was thinking once again of my brother." The thought of Tom's trusting faith had made her wonder if Morton was also trusting them to find a way to help him. "It just seems that something could be done."

"Let us hope desperate measures are not called for," Cavilon told her. "I would not care to think of you deciding to try to go to France and rescue him," he teased.

"If I were a man, I would do it," she returned.

"Elizabeth, such unladylike words. You must forgive her, my lord. She and her brother are very close," Lady Waddington told the comte.

"Of course," he nodded. "It is completely understandable. And may I ask," he said, smoothly changing the conversation once again, "have you both recovered from yesterday's exertions?"

Elizabeth heard the words as they flowed past her, but her mind remained on Cavilon's joking suggestion. How, she wondered, would one go about freeing a person from a French prison?

It is impossible, she scoffed, but the idea remained.

Chapter XVI

"Miss Jeffries." Niles came into the garden, where Elizabeth had gone to do some reading. "This was just brought to the door. Since Lady Waddington has returned to London and Sir Henry is gone for the day, I thought you might decide what is to be done. The person who brought it insists he will not leave without some answer."

Taking the letter upon Niles' tray, she broke the seal and scanned the heavy scrawl. Her eyes flew back to the beginning, and she began deciphering the script. "Tell the man to go to the Crown and Sword. He can get a mug of ale from the innkeeper by using my uncle's name. Tell him word will be sent to him as soon as possible."

"Yes, miss." Niles bowed and went to do as he had been instructed.

Elizabeth glanced over the letter. *How right I was to be concerned about Morton*, she thought, the unease that had plagued her since the arrival of her brother's letter a week past filling her mind. *This was written but three weeks past. There is hope help may reach Morton in time. At least this Captain Paraton—*

she looked at the signature at the bottom—*is attempting to care for him. Oh, if only I were a man. I would go to France,* she thought, then put the useless wish aside. *I must act quickly,* she decided. *What would it be best to do? If only Uncle were not gone. It will be late this eve when he returns. I must do something before then.*

"What if the man will not wait?" she said aloud as she rose. Her mind raced over whom she could go to today, now, and only one answer came forward. Cavilon.

But there is nothing he could do . . . or would do, she thought. *But he might,* echoed in her mind, and she returned indoors.

"Niles, have a mount readied for me," Elizabeth ordered, pausing on the stairs. Changing into a riding habit as quickly as possible, she came from the house just as a groom brought the horse to the door. Mounted, she headed to Tenbury.

Cavilon received word of Miss Jeffries' arrival with concealed surprise and ordered that she be taken to the library. "This is a most unexpected pleasure," he greeted her, his smile turning to concern as she faced him. "But you are distressed. What has happened?"

"A second letter has reached us from France. It came this afternoon," she explained. "It was written but three weeks past."

"It is not good news?"

"No." Elizabeth shook her head. "It was written for my brother by a Captain Paraton. I gather he is a fellow prisoner. He writes that Morton is very ill." Her hands fluttered; tears came to her eyes.

"Do sit down, Elizabeth." Cavilon was at her side at once. "I will get you a glass of Madeira."

"That is not necessary." She allowed him to lead her to a chair. Sitting, she continued. "Captain Paraton believes Morton has some kind of inflammation of the lungs complicated by a putrid fever. He says it is very serious. In fact, Morton may die; but," Elizabeth went on determinedly, "he says that if money can be sent at once, he may be able to bribe the guards to fetch a doctor."

"Does he propose how this is to be done?" Suspicion had entered the comte's eyes.

"The man who brought the message insisted that some answer be given. I instructed Niles to send him to the Crown and Sword to wait until he is sent for. Uncle Henry will not return until this eve, and I fear every moment may already be too late." She raised her eyes in quiet pleading. "Is there not something you could do?"

"I?" Cavilon tightened his affectious pose, driven by some invisible force to follow the course he had already set with this young woman. "But what could one such as I do?" He fluttered his kerchief.

Elizabeth rose, her distress increased. "I thought better of you," she told him in a firmly controlled voice. "I regret to learn I was incorrect."

"Mayhaps I may be able to do something," Cavilon said, stung by her look. "There is a man I know who may have information that would be helpful to you," he continued slowly. "Is there nothing else you can tell me? Where was your brother being held before the move?"

"The last we knew of was a prison near Rennes."

"Rennes? Yes," he mused. "I wish you to return to Ashly. Say nothing until you have word from me." Cavilon waved aside the objection she was about to voice. "There must be trust . . . just as when you asked that I assist you with the lad Tom."

"But if—"

"Let me speak with this man I know. Then we shall decide what must be done."

"When . . . how long do you think . . . ?"

"I shall call on you later this eve, in the morn at the latest."

"I pray you shall be successful," Elizabeth told him, doubt still lingering.

"As I also do." Cavilon took her arm and guided her towards the door. "You must trust me." His dark eyes held hers.

"Somehow . . . somehow I believe I do," she answered, held fast by his gaze. Abruptly she turned from him, hastening away from his look, his touch, which threatened to make her forget her brother's peril.

Watching her go, Cavilon tapped his cheek. Martin would have one more task to do, he decided, other than the matter begun a week past. Fromby would have to be put aside until this matter was resolved.

Halfway back to Ashly, Elizabeth realized that her reticule must have fallen to the floor when she sat in the library at Tenbury. In it was the letter from Captain Paraton. *I must have it to show Uncle Henry*, she thought, reining her mount to a halt. Turning about, she galloped back the way she had come.

The Tenbury butler was surprised to find Miss Jeffries returned when he answered the impatient pounding at the door. "Yes, miss?" he questioned.

"I would like to go to the library," Elizabeth told the stiff figure, his rigid disapproval making her forget the words she had thought to use.

"The Comte de Cavilon is with a visitor and has given specific instructions that nothing and no one is to disturb him," he told her coldly. "Perhaps you could call another time."

"But I do not wish to see the comte, only the library. He is not in the library?"

"No, miss."

"Then I shall just go there and fetch my reticule. I forgot it, quite by accident," she said, slipping past the butler.

He stared after her for a moment and then decided to return to his duties. Sir Henry was well known, and his niece was also spoken well of. It would not do to offer insult unnecessarily.

Tenbury was not an overly large manor house, but Elizabeth soon learned that it was confusingly arranged to so infrequent a visitor as herself. Taking a turn that she was certain led to the library, she found instead a short corridor. Hesitating near the end of it, she heard low voices coming from behind the door before her. Curiosity nudged her closer.

One voice she recognized as belonging to the comte, but the second was unfamiliar. *Perhaps this is the man he meant to speak to about Morton*, Elizabeth thought, and pressed an ear to the door.

"Then all has gone well in France?" she heard Cavilon question the other.

"Better than was first thought. The names you gave us are proving quite helpful, but several questions have arisen. The necessity of using your friend has been broached."

"That may now be possible," Cavilon agreed, "but perhaps not necessary. Let me see what you need to know."

Elizabeth frowned as his voice faded, and she could not hear clearly what was being said. She heard the rustle of paper, as if a map were being unrolled.

"It is important," the second voice became audible, "that your connections remain unsuspicious. It would not do for them to learn that you . . ." Again the voice became too faint to hear.

Questions tumbled over one another in Elizabeth's mind. What did this mean? Was the Comte de Cavilon some kind of spy? For England or for France? Was he to be trusted?

Padded footsteps straightened Elizabeth. She hurried to the end of the short corridor and hastened down the longer one, meeting the butler. "Oh, you found it," she smiled, seeing the reticule in his hand. "How kind of you to fetch it. I must go. Could you show me the way to the door?"

"Yes, Miss Jeffries," the butler answered icily, motioning her to go before him.

"Thank you," she said when they reached the doors,

and gladly hastened from his condemning stare, relieved that the man had not informed the comte of her return.

Back at Ashly she pondered what to do. "Oh, why did I ever go to Cavilon?" she questioned aloud as she paced about her room. "And what do I tell Uncle Henry when he returns? What sense can be made from all this?" She paused before her mirror. "What did I hear . . . was it really anything? Can he be trusted?"

The creak of her door caused Elizabeth to whirl about. A weak laugh of relief came from her as Barney appeared. "Where have you been?" she scolded, picking at the twigs and burrs in his fur. "We are a pair," she murmured, "galloping off where we should never go. What did you do, I wonder?" She stroked his woolly fur absentmindedly. "What am I to do?"

The Comte de Cavilon arrived at Ashly house shortly after Sir Henry's return. His affectation had once more become pronounced, although Elizabeth, greatly disturbed by all that had happened, did not notice it. Her alarm grew as the comte asked to speak with her uncle alone. After an hour, which seemed more like a day, she was summoned to join them.

Both men rose as Elizabeth entered her uncle's office. Sir Henry's face was grave as he bade her take a seat. "My lord Cavilon has told me what he has learned in regard to the possibility of locating Morton. I find what he suggests in exchange for his assistance in this matter very distressing. Only you, however, can give the answer, my dear. I do not approve of this, and I feel your brother would not, but I must let the decision to you," he told his puzzled niece. "My lord." He nodded to the comte and withdrew.

Elizabeth looked to Cavilon, greatly bewildered. A look which she thought to be doubt crossed his features, then was gone.

"If I were to offer for your hand in marriage, would you consent?" he asked.

"This is no time to speak of such matters. My brother may be dying."

"What would your answer be?" Cavilon insisted, his lace fluttering to his chin as he poised a finger on his cheek.

"I do not think we would . . . suit. The answer would be no," Elizabeth told him coldly.

"I then wish you to listen to all that I have to say before you give me an answer." Cavilon lowered his hand. "Twice you have rejected me, and twice you have asked me for aid." His eyes dropped to her hands, now tightly clenched, and he receded into his affectations with greater force. "The first matter, that of the lad, was trivial and I asked nothing in return. But your brother presents a difficult problem. I have spoken with the man I told you of. He is agreeable to going to France and locating your brother but insists that your brother's only chance of surviving is to be rescued. This man knows the prisons from experience." He paused, then rose. Turning away from Elizabeth, he continued, "The danger in such an attempt is very great, especially as your brother is ill. Thus the price demanded is equally great, a price which your uncle cannot pay. However, I," he turned back to her, "am willing to meet the expense if you are agreeable to my terms."

"Which are?" Elizabeth questioned, her eyes not leaving his.

"That you consent to be my wife."

"Shall you go with this man to France?"

"And risk death or worse? No, *ma petite*." He shook his head. "You must know me for what I am."

"Have you ever done anything yourself? Is your wealth always to purchase what you wish to have?" she asked bitterly. "You are no man . . ."

"That is not the question," Cavilon coldly cut her off. "I do not think either of us wishes to play games. I do not attempt to deceive you. I wish you to be my wife."

"I do not understand you."

"If I had arranged for your brother's release and then asked for your hand, you might have given your consent out of gratitude. But I have no desire to have you come to me under any pretense. If you do not come for love, then it shall be because you have given your word. Honour, I have found, is more binding than gratitude."

"And you would wed me even if I said I hated you?"

"An honourable person is rarely totally unreasonable," he answered, approaching her.

"I find you despicable."

"Your answer?"

"I have little choice," she murmured.

"I have your pledge?"

Elizabeth raised her eyes to his. "It is as you wish."

He took her hand and kissed it lightly. "Would you have me tell you I do this for love?" he wondered aloud. "I have had love and would rather choose honour. You may one day understand. I must go now. There are arrangements to be made." Cavilon paused as if expecting her to speak. She said nothing, and he left her.

Tears clouded Elizabeth's vision. Two men had touched her heart: one she would never know; the other she could now never love.

Chapter XVII

Worry over her brother's condition forced Elizabeth to put aside her own cares. The decision to wed Cavilon had been made; there was no longer any reason to think of it as anything but an accomplished fact. Her mind turned to her brother's plight, which was so uncertain. The idea that Cavilon had unknowingly planted with his jest became the center of her thoughts. Elizabeth attacked each obstacle that stood against her going to France with the same tenacity she had used to maintain her father's home as a young girl and to keep it after his death.

Early on the morn after the pact with Cavilon had been agreed to, she went down to breakfast prepared to begin her plotted enterprise.

Sir Henry, still uneasy about the agreement reached between his niece and the comte, came to the breakfast room reluctantly and was surprised to find Elizabeth eating heartily.

"Good morn, Uncle," she smiled. "Did the Comte de Cavilon say when he would call this morn?"

"I . . . why, yes." He joined her at the table. "In about an hour."

"Then I had best hurry so that I am ready."

"You are quite in the best of looks, my dear," Sir Henry assured her. "There is no need to change your gown. I believe the Comte de Cavilon wishes only to bid you farewell before going to Folkestone and completing all the arrangements for Morton's . . . rescue."

"I do not mean to change my attire but to finish my packing," Elizabeth returned lightly.

"But you cannot mean to leave?" Surprise filled her uncle's face.

"My visit has been a prolonged one, Uncle, and you knew I did not mean to come permanently. I will feel more at ease awaiting Morton's arrival at our home in Folkestone, and being there is, after all, eminently practical. If Morton is ill, as we know he is, it will be much better to nurse him in our home there rather than travel the additional miles," she explained.

"You always have your head about you, Elizabeth," he nodded, his pride in her evident. "You are quite right. But I insist you return here to be wed."

A shadow flitted across her face. "To please you, Uncle," she agreed, her eyes going to her plate.

"Perhaps it would be more agreeable for you if you were to delay taking your leave for a few days. Morton cannot be returned to us in so brief a time, and I would gladly send you home in my coach."

"I do not mind going with the comte. Indeed, I must become accustomed to it, mustn't I," Elizabeth told him, laying her napkin aside and rising. "Please call me if his lordship arrives before I come down."

"Yes, my dear. You do not regret your decision? I

fear the sum named was far beyond my powers," he told her gruffly.

Elizabeth went to him and brushed his face with a kiss. "Do not worry, Uncle Henry. Have you not always said I could manage no matter what?" She smiled reassuringly.

"Mayhaps you would wish me to come with you?"

"No, it will be good for me to have some time alone."

A single portmanteau was brought to Elizabeth's room. The young abigail, Spense, hovered over it, neatly folding and packing the few garments that her mistress had laid upon the bed. "Miss, aren't you going to take even one of your new gowns?" she asked.

"I will have no need of them if I . . . while I am awaiting my brother's arrival," Elizabeth corrected the near slip of her tongue. "The day dresses I left there are sufficient for my needs."

"Could I not go with you, miss? I can cook and would not mind some cleaning chores." The abigail stood before her hopefully.

"No, I would like to have this time to myself before . . . before I wed. It would please me, though, if you would come with me after my marriage."

"Oh, yes, miss. I would be most happy to." Spense beamed at her.

"Good. I believe that is all I shall need. Please take the portmanteau and set it in the corridor so it is ready when the comte arrives. I do not wish to cause any delay." Picking up her gloves and bonnet, she followed the abigail from the room.

Niles was admitting Cavilon just as Elizabeth reached the bottom of the stairs. "Good morn, my lord," she greeted him briskly.

Meeting her as they both walked forward, the comte took her hand and pressed a kiss to it. "You are looking very well this morn," he told her in a tone that suggested he had not thought to find her so.

"Thank you, my lord."

"Could we not speak privately before you depart?" Cavilon questioned, motioning at her gloves and bonnet.

"We may go to the small salon," Elizabeth told him, stepping towards it. "Tell Sir Henry that my lord Cavilon has arrived," she instructed Niles as they passed him. When alone in the salon, she turned to the comte, determination clearly written on her features. "I am not about to go out, my lord. I mean to go with you."

"That is not necessary. I prefer that you remain here with your family," he told her, his hands fluttering dismissal of the idea.

"You are going to Folkestone to make arrangements for my brother's return," Elizabeth told him evenly. "As I have agreed to your terms, I believe I have a part in those plans."

"You do not trust me to make them?" He cocked an eyebrow, a faint smile coming to his lips.

"Let us say that I would be . . . comforted by taking some small part in them. Also, I wish to ready my brother's home for his return. Should he need nursing, as Captain Paraton's letter strongly suggests, it will be better to have a bed awaiting him rather than force him to travel the additional miles to Ashly," Elizabeth said, forcing her eyes to meet Cavilon's challenge. "It would also enable me to prepare for our . . . wedding, my lord."

"A most suitable idea." He sniffed daintily into his kerchief. "But I dislike leaving you alone, and I do not plan to remain in Folkestone once the matter is settled and the ship has left. There is much I myself must see to before we wed."

"I did not intend to suggest you remain at my side. The details I must see to are not for the bridegroom's eyes," she answered, a quiet triumph rising within as she felt him waver.

"Good morn, my lord." Sir Henry joined the two. "Is all ready?"

"Yes, I believe so. Elizabeth is insisting she come with me. Is this with your blessing, sir?"

"She knows what is best for her."

"Then we are ready to depart." Cavilon nodded at her. "I will arrange that word be sent to you when the ship leaves the harbour and, of course, when it returns." His attention went to Sir Henry. "My man has suggested it could be a brief week, then again much longer, depending on complications."

Sir Henry nodded. He embraced his niece, brushing her cheek with a kiss. "All will be right in the end," he said with a smile.

"I pray only that Morton is still alive and the venture proves successful," she answered. Returning his kiss, she hurried from the salon.

"All that can be done for your nephew's safe return

shall be," Cavilon told Sir Henry before following her.

Walking to the comte's coach, Elizabeth was greeted enthusiastically by Barney.

"Your eager guardian," Cavilon frowned, keeping his distance from the beast. "La, *oui*, a perfect solution. We shall take the animal with us."

"Oh, no, my lord. Tom would be heartbroken to find him gone when he returns," Elizabeth protested.

"Sir Henry, have my agent bring the lad on to Folkestone when they arrive here," the comte told her uncle. "Put the beast on the box," he ordered the dubious footmen.

Barney decided they were playing a game of tag with him as they sought to get a good hold, and led them on a chase.

"You see, my lord, it would be best if he stayed here." Elizabeth's hopes rose.

Having noted the stricken look with which she greeted his idea that the dog accompany them only fortified Cavilon's intent to have the animal taken. An inner sense told him Elizabeth was plotting something and that she considered the dog a hindrance. His footmen, however, were proven incapable of cornering the animal. Elizabeth's pleasure in the scene proved her downfall. Walking to the coach, the comte opened the door and whistled. Barney halted in his tracks, cocked his head, then ran forward, clambering into the coach. "The animal has developed high taste under your tutelage," he told Elizabeth as the footman handed her in.

Suppressing the desire to choke the wretched beast, she sat opposite him and began planning anew.

For the greater part of their journey, conversation was sparse. Each was preoccupied with his own thoughts and I did not notice the silence. It was only when they reached the outskirts of Folkestone and Barney took to barking at the passing carriages that both became more attentive.

"It was your idea to bring him," Elizabeth laughed when Cavilon rolled his eyes.

Barney stood on the seat and barked out the coach window.

"See what I endure for your sake," he returned with a wry grin. "I shall leave you at your home and proceed to the dock," he added.

"Could I not go with you?" Elizabeth begged. "I am certain I can get Barney to behave." She leaned forward and took hold of his collar. "Sit, boy," she told him and was relieved to see him do it. "See, he will be the perfect gentleman."

"My dear, I disdain the adventure already. Why, only the gravity of the situation has compelled me to permit my person to go among such low individuals," Cavilon drawled. "I certainly cannot allow my future wife to."

"But I would be satisfied to remain in the coach," she assured him. "It would please me greatly." Elizabeth reached out and touched his hand while her eyes implored him.

"As you wish, *ma petite*," Cavilon murmured, his instincts urging refusal, but his heart giving in to her persuasion. "But you *must* remain inside. The men that shall be about the dock are not accustomed to ladies of your genteel birth. You must remember that soon you shall be a comtesse."

"Yes, my lord," she answered demurely, lowering her eyes to keep from betraying herself.

Tapping on the roof of the coach, Cavilon ordered the coachman to the docks.

With official trade and travel between the two countries facing each other across the Channel officially forbidden, Elizabeth was surprised at the number of ships and the great activity in the harbour. She scanned the scene eagerly, questioning the comte as to which ship would be the one used, but his answers were evasive.

When the coach halted at his command, Cavilon stepped down with a final admonition for Elizabeth to remain inside. His progress along the wharf drew marked attention from the stevedores and sailors. Whoops and catcalls followed his every step.

After waiting several minutes, Elizabeth took a firm hold on Barney's collar and opened the coach door. The startled footman helped her down.

"But, Miss Jeffries," he protested, "The Comte de Cavilon did not wish you to—"

"I shall be well guarded," she said, motioning to the beast at her side, and hurried past the footman. *For once, my lord*, she thought, *your toilet is a great benefit. You are perfectly visible*. The comte's ornate figure was easily seen but, not daring to get too close lest she be noticed, Elizabeth followed at a distance that kept him barely in sight. When he halted before one of the smaller sloops and began speaking with a man who came off it, she tried to note its position carefully for later reference. Satisfied, she turned to go back to the coach, but Barney had a different idea. Having spied a rat, he lunged forward, breaking from her hold and disappearing among the stacks of barrels and bales.

"Barney! Barney, come back!" Elizabeth tried to follow him but was blocked by the jumble of cargo. "Lord, now what?" She looked about, trying to spy him, and saw that Cavilon was returning. After taking a few steps towards the coach, Elizabeth halted. She would not desert the animal she had promised to care for.

"We had agreed that you remain in the coach," the comte greeted her sternly, a scowl coming to his features.

"Barney has escaped from me," she answered. "We must find him."

"That is impossible. The animal knows how to care for himself. When Tom arrives, bring him here and the beast will show himself." He took her arm and led her to the coach. When they were seated within it, he spoke. "The matter is completed. He shall leave this eve."

"Will you do nothing to find Barney?" Elizabeth's guilty conscience bent her anger toward him.

"He will come to the lad," Cavilon assured her. "You are fatigued from the journey and will feel better after you have rested."

"As you say, my lord." She forced her mind back to the larger problem. "Do you leave for London soon?"

"I fear I must go this eve," Cavilon answered. "Are you certain you do not wish to return to your uncle?"

"I could not, not with Barney lost. There is no reason for you to worry. I am accustomed to being left to myself." Elizabeth tried to ease the curtness of her voice.

Silence fell once again and remained until they stood alone inside the small parlour of her family home.

"You see, I shall have much to occupy me," she told Cavilon, motioning at the dust covers on all the furniture.

"Then I shall take my leave. I ask you to trust that all that can be done to free your brother and bring him safely home will be done."

The earnestness in his eyes struck a tender note in Elizabeth. The retort that had come to mind was put aside. "I do," she answered. "I wish you a safe journey."

"Thank you, *ma petite*." Cavilon kissed her hand and then reached out to touch her cheek. A quixotic mood came over him. "My kerchief." He drew his lace square from his jacket and pressed it into her hand. "For you to hold dear till I return."

Elizabeth accepted it, wondering at his words. "Shall you return before the ship is expected?"

"No, I shall await word of its return. If the attempt to save your brother is not successful, you shall not see me again." Bowing with an elaborate flourish, he turned and walked away.

Stunned by his words, Elizabeth stared after him. An impulse to run after the comte was pushed aside.

"How curious a man he is," she murmured as the door closed behind him. Shrugging the mood away, she untied her bonnet and removed her gloves. "There is much I have to do," she said aloud, and walked towards her brother's chamber. Entering it, Elizabeth went to the wardrobe and rummaged through it. After removing a pair of breeches, a shirt, hose, and boots, she hurried to her own bedchamber.

Chapter XVIII

Pressing his seal into the soft wax, Cavilon felt somewhat easier. If he did not return, the letter would explain all to Elizabeth. He motioned Leveque forward. "I have decided to remain at Folkestone," he informed the valet. "I wish you to take these letters to Lord Tretain in London." The comte placed the missive he had just sealed with two others in the slim leather case. "When you have done this, go to my London apartments and ready them for my return."

"But my lord, how shall you manage here . . . alone?"

"There are times when one must sacrifice one's personal comfort." Cavilon fluttered his lace. "The coach awaits you." He waved dismissal. He paced impatiently until he was certain the coach had departed, anxious to begin. Certain that Leveque was gone, Cavilon left the inn in a hired landaulet. Ordering it halted in a busier section of Folkestone, he motioned for two young lads to come to him. A brief conversation was held. Several guineas were given them, along with an address, and Cavilon reentered the landaulet and ordered the driver on. When it halted before a small house he had rented on a previous trip, the comte paid the driver, dismissing him, and disappeared into it, drawing as little attention as possible.

In less than an hour the lads came hurrying to Cavilon's door, bearing several packages. Taking them and expressing his thanks with a generous amount of coin, the comte sent them away. Back in his room he changed into the rough garments in the packages. A quick scrubbing removed all trace of powder and rouge. He smeared his face lightly with ash from the fireplace, all hint of affectation gone. Transformed to Martin, he then left the house by way of the back entry and hurried to procure the few other essentials the journey before him required.

In the early evening half-light, Martin entered a tavern in the wharf district. He greeted several of the men within by name and exchanged local gossip before taking a mug of ale and sitting at a table near the door. An hour went by while he idly visited with those who passed by his table. When a large, weathered sea captain strode in, Martin hailed him and called for two mugs of ale.

"Hattern, I thought mayhaps my message failed to reach you," he said as the other roughly pulled a stool to the table and deposited his bulk on it.

"When 'ave ye known me ta fail ta come," the rough captain grinned broadly. " 'Tis been several new moons since ye've been seen."

"The excise men took too great a liking to me," Martin answered. "That night we landed they had men waiting inland. That was when I decided they needed a rest." He laughed and raised his mug, offering an uncomplimentary toast to the king's men.

"'Eard ye been askin' after that Lord Fromby," Hattern said, leaning forward.

"I've my reasons. Do you know anything that would interest me?" Martin glanced around. "Let us speak as we go to the *Tigress*. It's time we were on our way."

"Aye, there's a fair wind risin'. Should be a good crossin' if the moon don't betray us. Course if 'is lordship's sloop be plyin' the waters, the patrols tend ta stay away." He winked and finished his ale before rising and following the other's lead.

"You think there are excise men helping him?"

"'Tis a common fact," the other returned.

"What do you think the man is about?" Martin asked. "There seem to be many different rumours and none completely creditable."

"Aye, 'is lordship 'as played it close till now. Of late 'e's gotten careless. 'Is sort usually do. Now 'e's seen openly on the docks and few believe it's 'is love fer 'is sloop or the sea that brings 'im. The cargo's brought ashore in 'is name and be labeled 'salt pork' or 'salt beef,' but I'd eat the manifest afore I'd believe it."

"I have heard that his ship does not go empty to France."

"So 'tis said, but I and mine 'ave nothin' ta do with that. We're as honest as the times let us be. What is it ye be doin' that ye go so openly to France this time?" Hattern's craggy visage studied the younger man closely.

"A favour for a friend. He wants a young man removed from a French prison. There may be a problem in it, for I'm not yet certain which prison, but we'll head for the Sillon de Talbert. With luck, in three or four days I should be ready to be picked up as usual."

"If we 'ave ta return more'n twice, it'll be bloody dangerous," the older man noted, rubbing the rough stubble on his chin.

"Has it not always been worth your while?" Martin questioned. "With luck there will be no problems. Besides, you know you love to teach those French corvettes how to sail."

"Ye be a fine one ta be speakin' so free. Think ye them French will greet ye with open arms? How many times 'ave ye come poundin' ta the shore with a pack o' them on yer heels? Lucky ye always manage ta steal the faster horse." Hattern clapped him on the back, laughing.

"Let us hope we've more time to spare than that," Martin returned, realizing the difficulty of transferring an ill and weakened man to the coast, let alone from the shore to the sloop.

"If ye ken get the lad past the prison walls and ta the coast, we'll get 'im ta England," the captain assured him.

Martin nodded. This was not the time to doubt that he could, that either of them could do it.

The day dragged slowly to an end for Elizabeth. Myriad questions about what she was planning to do plagued her, filling her with doubt. *Would it not be best to trust this man Cavilon has hired?* she wondered. *You could easily prove to be more a hindrance than a help.*

But what if Morton is dreadfully ill? she countered. *He will need nursing. More importantly,* she concluded at last, *if I am there he could not be left behind if the one sent to rescue him decided the risk was too great. Morton means nothing to the man; it would be easy for him to lie about what took place. My presence will prevent that.*

The weight of this argument stiffened Elizabeth's resolve. Recalling how she had sailed with her brother when they were children, she assured herself of her ability to be of help. Only Barney's absence plagued her, and at last she sat down and wrote a note of explanation to Tom and a second to Cavilon's agent, who would be bringing the boy, instructing that they take rooms at a local inn until further orders, and telling them to search for the dog on the piers. This done, she took the letters to her neighbor, asking that they be delivered when the lad arrived.

Returning to the house, Elizabeth wrote a letter to Sir Henry which could be found if she did not return from her journey. With it completed, she left the cottage once more to purchase food and a few basic medicines to take with her. At home again, she readied the clothing she had decided to take and packed what she had purchased with them in the old canvas duffel bag her brother had used when he had first gone to school at Portsmouth.

The afternoon lengthened sufficiently at last. Elizabeth exchanged her gown for her brother's garments, taking some time to stuff the oversized boots with extra socks until they were snug enough to permit her to walk freely without losing them. Pinning her hair up, she pulled one of his old sailor hats over it and then, even though the summer heat made it uncomfortable, she drew on one of Morton's lighter coats. Satisfied with her appearance, she picked up the duffel bag and walked determinedly from the cottage, going in the direction of the line of masts and sails which marked the harbour.

The walk from her home to dockside bolstered Elizabeth's spirits, for no one took note of her, seeing—as she had hoped—only a young lad returning to his ship. It was near dark when she found herself among the crates and bales heaped all about the wharf. Looking for the ship she had noted Cavilon at earlier in the day, her heart sank. One ship looked much like another in the dusky light. Scrambling over the bales of hemp and coils of rope, Elizabeth saw no ship that she could mark with certainty. A sinking feeling settled in her stomach as she continued to wander through the maze of cargoes. In her concentration she did not see the sailors approaching her, and she stumbled against one.

"What 'ave we 'ere?" he laughed, grabbing hold her arm.

"Why a lad as 'ale and 'earty as our cap'n could ever want. Bet yer quick among the riggin's, eh lad?" a second taunted. "What be yer ship?" he demanded.

"Answer," the one who held her demanded, shaking her roughly.

"Who cares what ship 'e's supposed ta be on," the other laughed.

"Let's take 'im," a third agreed. "If'n we don't find 'nough men, the capt'n'll have our hides on the yardarms."

Terror welled inside Elizabeth. They meant to press her into duty. "No," she struggled, kicking out at the one who held her. "Let go of me," she screamed, hoping someone would hear and come to her rescue.

"Fine speakin' fer a seagoin' lad," he snorted. "Ye'll soon learn 'umbler ways."

"You can't take me," she protested, realizing how futile her action was. "Help! Help me!" she screamed with all her might.

The sailor who held her slapped her sharply across the face and raised his hand to strike her again.

A white blur exploded from the shadows.

"Barney!" Elizabeth cried out as the dog's jaws closed over the sailor's arm.

Turning to fend off the attack, the man released his hold. Elizabeth fell to the ground, grabbed the duffel bag, and scrambled to her feet away from him, calling to Barney as soon as she had reached a fair distance. After a last angry bark, he raced after her. Both were hotly pursued by the three sailors.

The maze of cargo and supplies was a hindrance and a help as they ran and stumbled through it, slowly drawing away from the three. Out of breath, Elizabeth paused before the gangway of a sloop; Barney halted at her side.

Hearing the men coming, she dashed up the planks, ducking behind some barrels on deck to avoid being seen by one of the crew who was emerging from the hold at that moment. Crouched low, she wrapped an arm about Barney's thick, white neck and used both hands to muzzle him lest he betray them by barking. When the crewman was out of sight, she grabbed the dog's collar and dashed for the hold. Low-burning lamps lit the way as she passed by the captain's cabin and crew's quarters. Going a deck lower, she found herself in the ship's supply hold.

In the darkness she could see little. Feeling a large coil of rope, she crouched behind it and wrapped an arm about Barney, listening for any sound of pursuit.

"Thank the lord for you," she patted him appreciatively. "We'll wait until it is safe and then go directly home. I was foolish to think I could manage to find the right ship." Resting her head against the dog's woolly back, Elizabeth closed her eyes. The sounds of footsteps above her stiffened her. "Only the ship's crew," she whispered. "We must wait just a little longer," she told Barney, sitting on the canvas bag she still held and making him lie down. Leaning against the coil of rope, she rested. "Just a few more minutes," she murmured, patting the huge dog. The past two days' activity, combined with a restless night, claimed their due. Relaxing, Elizabeth slowly drifted to sleep.

Reluctantly, Elizabeth's senses were prodded to consciousness by a loud, incessant sound echoing in her ears. Her benumbed senses sought to grasp what the sound was as signals of cramped and damp discomfort filtered through the haze in her mind. The realization that she was hearing barking collided with the comprehension of the rolling motion of the floor beneath her. Before there was any chance for her to act, a lantern was thrust into the hold. Blinking at the light, Elizabeth stumbled to her feet. Barney abandoned his pursuit of the rat which had aroused him and took up guard before his mistress.

"Two stowaways, cap'n," the sailor yelled back through the door. Coming in, he drew his knife.

Bristling, Barney gave a deep, threatening growl.

Elizabeth hurried to grab hold his collar. "You . . . you don't need that weapon," she said shakily. "I meant no harm in coming here. Just let us go."

"Do ye mean ta swim the Channel, lad?" Captain Hattern scoffed, ducking his head as he entered. "How did ye come ta be aboard with no one knowin' it?"

The gentle roll of the ship had brought an uneasy queasiness to Elizabeth's stomach. Swallowing hard, she tried to explain. "Three men . . . sailors, tried to . . . to force me to go with them. I ran away and hid here."

"And where did you get that dog?" a deep voice behind the captain demanded.

Barney gave a bark of recognition at the tall, dark figure. He tugged against Elizabeth's hold.

"No, Barney," she scolded.

Martin's eyes sharply studied the figure holding the dog. They narrowed and darkened as the truth hit him. "I thought I was to be your only passenger," he said, covering his shock with anger.

"Stowaways." Hattern glanced over his shoulder, surprised at the other's tone, taken aback by the man's unexpected black look. "The lad can be of no 'arm ta yer plans, Martin," he noted.

194

The name drew a gasp from Elizabeth, turning all back to her and her companion.

Hattern moved forward, halting only when Barney bared his teeth and let loose a deep rumble. The captain pulled a pistol from his belt, eyeing the huge animal.

"Please," Elizabeth begged, "don't shoot him."

"Put your piece aside," Martin ordered. "I'll speak with this lad, but let's get out of this damp hole," he said, walking up to Elizabeth.

She shrank from his dark scowl, pulling her hand away when his closed over Barney's collar.

"You'll not be harmed," Martin told her. "Follow me."

To Elizabeth's surprise, Barney wagged his tail and followed the man willingly. She edged around Captain Hattern, her legs threatening to collapse as the queasiness of her stomach menaced triumph. Fear and uncertainty added to the already churning sensation, and she paled.

Glancing back, Martin saw the sickening hue of her face and shoved Barney into the closest cabin, locking the door before taking hold of Elizabeth's arm. He dragged her roughly along the corridor, pausing outside the captain's door. "I'll speak to the lad alone," he told Hattern, who was following.

"Back ta yer duties," the captain ordered the few sailors who had gathered. With a man like Martin, experience had taught him, it was best not to question.

Chapter XIX

Closing the door behind him, Martin shoved Elizabeth towards the small window in the cabin and threw it open. "I should have you thrown into the sea," he snapped.

Elizabeth drew in deep gulps of air and prayed that her stomach would recede from so close to her throat.

"The only thing that saves you from such a fate is that the Comte de Cavilon would not appreciate it, Miss Jeffries." He reached up and pulled the cap from her head, eyeing her speculatively.

"How do you know my name? What have you to do with the Comte de Cavilon?" Some of Elizabeth's temper returned as she became accustomed to the roll of the ship.

"Is it not your brother, Morton Jeffries, that I am being sent to liberate?"

"*You*? This is the ship?" She stared unbelievingly.

"I am interested only in how you came to be aboard this sloop." Martin stepped towards her, and she backed until the wall stopped her. He placed one hand against it just above her right shoulder.

"I . . . I told the captain . . . There were some sailors chasing me and I hid here."

"Is it a common practice of yours to run through the docks dressed thusly?" He leaned closer, his other hand going against the wall by her left shoulder.

Elizabeth's heart pounded in her ears as her gaze was held by Martin's dark, glistening eyes. She sensed his anger and shrank from him.

"I wonder, does Cavilon know you have come?" Martin cocked his head. "What are we to do with you, my pretty?" he asked with the assurance of a man who knew exactly what he wished of his women and had never been refused.

Fear receded. Anger at his manner towards her rose. Elizabeth lifted her chin proudly, yet knew not how to combat him.

"A pity I must send you back to England," he noted sarcastically.

"Must you?" she snapped haughtily. "Then you do not intend to do what Cavilon has paid for?"

"Your brother will be freed."

"Then let me come. I could be useful," she told him earnestly.

"Entertaining, perhaps, my pretty, or amusing, but hardly useful." Martin's smile chilled her.

Elizabeth lowered her eyes. They landed on the pistol in his belt, and she forced a smile to her lips and raised her face to his. Slowly, she put her arms about his waist.

Anger blazed into Martin's eyes at her movement, then disappeared when he realized what she was about.

His hand closed over hers when she reached for the pistol. Pulling the arm behind him, he drew Elizabeth against him. "That would not be wise," he laughed softly, then pressed his lips to hers.

Shock froze her momentarily; then she realized she must actively resist the feelings his caressing lips evoked. Anger against him, against herself, rose. She struck him forceably with her free hand when he drew back.

Immediately her hand was caught in a crushing hold.

"I did not want you to misunderstand," she told him, her chin raised proudly, her eyes defiant and unafraid. "Now remove your hands."

"Why?"

"Because the Comte de Cavilon would not be pleased," she said, uttering the first thought that came to mind.

"And you wish me to believe he knows you are here?" Martin cocked his head, his disbelief apparent.

"How else would I know which ship to hide in?" Elizabeth lied unflinchingly.

"The comte is more a woman than I thought," he sneered.

"My hands." Elizabeth ignored his words.

"And what do you mean to do?" he asked, slowly releasing her.

"Go with you, of course. It is my brother, after all."

"This is no journey for a woman. I will not risk my life by being burdened with yours. You will be taken back to Folkestone. Now put this on and keep it on." He snatched the cap from where it had fallen and threw it at her. "And remain in this cabin if you don't want to encounter someone who doesn't care what Cavilon thinks," Martin added and left.

Elizabeth walked slowly to the captain's chair and sank into it weakly. She raised a hand to still her pulsing heart. Never had anyone kissed her like that. Not even Cavilon's gentle embrace had produced such an effect within her being. The arrogant, swaggering strength of the man angered her, and she found it difficult to believe that this was the same man who had stolen into her coach that March night, now so far in the past.

Why has fate brought me to this ship? Elizabeth questioned. *Thank God I am to go back*, she thought, sensing that to go on with him was to dare more danger than she had ever thought to encounter. But would Morton be rescued by such a man as this? How could she be certain?

On deck Martin stood staring at the rising sea. Elizabeth's presence had been a true shock, unusual for a man accustomed to viewing nothing as a surprise. It was also a complication which showed him with too great a clarity for his peace of mind just how deeply she had affected him.

The sting of her hand upon his face echoed through his mind. There had yet to be a woman who could long resist his good looks and steady persuasion; to keep Elizabeth with him, his arrogant confidence told him, would be to add her to their number.

But would it? another inner voice questioned. The temptation to test her beckoned, but his love refused to permit the danger of the journey to her, to risk his heart. Conflicting thoughts tossed about in his mind like the waves now dashing into whitecaps, striving to drive the sloop from its course.

Captain Hattern came to his side, a slicker warding off the spray the wind was blowing over the deck. "A ship 'as been spied just on the 'orizon. She'll see us soon if she 'asn't already. Should we run for the open sea, or do ye still want to try fer Talbert? We are nearing it now."

"Keep on course."

"Cap'n, there be two corvettes with the ship," a sailor cried, running up to the pair. The rumble of cannonade sounded.

"Must be one o' ours. Ready the guns," Hattern bellowed.

"I go to land on my own," Martin told him. "Keep the lad with you until you can get him to Folkestone. I want no harm to come to him. Your word?"

"Aye."

"Land close by," a voice called out.

"Ready the dinghy," Martin called out and dashed to collect his gear.

Below deck in the captain's cabin Elizabeth was disturbed by the sound of the cannonade. The increase in the wind was evident from the pitch of the flooring beneath her feet. She ran from the cabin and scrambled up the stairs. The cold wind caused her to pause, to pull the cap tightly about her ears, and to button the light coat. All about her men were running to and fro in answer to shouted orders.

"What's happening?" She put out a hand to stay a sailor who was rushing by.

"French corvettes pursuing an English ship," he answered, hurrying past.

"Get below deck!" Martin loomed suddenly before her.

"Is that France?" she shouted, pointing to the black hulk of land standing against the glistening waves.

"Yes."

"The dinghy is ready, sir," a sailor called to him.

"You'd better hurry," the captain joined them.

Elizabeth scurried towards the stairs.

"Keep him below deck," Martin shouted, running to where the dinghy was being lowered over the side into the heaving sea. Climbing down the rope ladder, he dropped into it, then caught the canvas bag a sailor tossed over the side.

Returning from the hold, where she retrieved the duffel bag, Elizabeth moved as quickly as she dared across the windswept, slippery deck, making her way to a group of sailors who were leaning over the side. She gulped, seeing the tossing waves, then her eyes lit on Martin working at the ropes that held the dinghy against the ship. Giving herself no time to think, she tossed the duffel bag over the side into the small boat, and, after a moment's hesitation, gripped the ropes and slipped over the side, dangling in the air above the churning sea.

A shout from those above raised Martin's head just as he loosened and released the last rope holding the dinghy. Lunging, he grabbed Elizabeth as she fell, saving her from dropping into the sea and throwing both to the bottom of the boat. The dinghy swirled away from the *Tigress*. The sailors above it scurried to man the guns as Hattern turned the sloop to engage the corvettes.

Martin swore angrily as he untangled himself from Elizabeth and put the oars in place. The danger of the moment claimed all his attention as he put his back to them, stoking hard. Bright flashes of fire showed the struggle of the four ships. Elizabeth watched them slowly disappear beyond the horizon, then turned to watch the ever nearing land.

The moment the dinghy touched the beach, Martin leaped out, shouting for her to do the same. "Pull," he ordered, taking hold of the small boat.

They dragged it from the water and worked it onto the sandy beach. When they were fifty feet from the water's edge, he stopped pushing and looked about. A hundred feet to one side and a little farther ahead was a sandy outcrop the wind had gradually swept the sand from, forming a half-cave. Martin motioned that they should conceal the dinghy there.

By the time they maneuvered it into the hollow below the outcrop, Elizabeth was panting for breath and her hands were rubbed raw. She flinched from the angry look of contempt Martin flashed her as he threw her duffel bag and his own from the boat. "Give me that coat. Now find branches, brush of any sort," he ordered, tossing the jacket into the dinghy.

Stung by his disdain, Elizabeth began to collect what was to be found washed up on the beach. Not a word was exchanged as they worked to cover the boat.

Satisfied with the degree of camouflage, Martin paused to get his bearings. They were to have landed near the Sillon de Talbert with Treguier to the south. Captain Hattern's expertise could be depended upon. Seeing that dawn was about to break, he knew they must get inland. Drawing a French *jacquette* from his bag, he tossed it to Elizabeth. "Cover that English tunic and follow me," he ordered curtly, picking up the bag and kicking hers towards her.

For the first time she noticed that he wore the simple clothing demanded by the revolution, the French culotte and plain shirt, clothing which would be the same as all they encountered, she realized as she shrugged into the *jacquette* and followed him. It did not take long to realize he was setting a relentless pace.

If only I had brought my own walking boots, Elizabeth thought as she tramped along determinedly, trying to ignore the blisters on her hands and the growing throb in her feet. *If only you had remained safely at home*, her conscience added, shaming the anger she felt for the broad-shouldered man moving ever farther ahead of her.

Trying to distract herself, Elizabeth began taking in the rich, undulating plain and low-rising hills of Brittany before them. Brush and trees increased steadily as they progressed, and the soft tramp of their feet was joined by the song of birds and the looing of grazing cattle as the sun warmed the air.

By the end of the second hour the young woman was hot, tired, thirsty, and belligerent. Stumbling on the root of a tree, Elizabeth fell to her knees, began to rise, but let herself down. The growling of her stomach reminded her that she had not eaten since late afternoon of the previous day. Sitting, she opened her duffel bag and searched out a hunk of cheese and a loaf of bread. She was happily munching away when Martin came back, looking to see what had happened to her. "Would you care for some?" she asked as he towered angrily above her.

Snatching the bread, he fumed, swallowing the words he had meant to say. He took the cheese Elizabeth offered and became aware of her reddened, perspiration-covered face. "Hrrummph!" Martin snorted and began pacing back and forth as he ate. Drawing a flask from the canvas bag on his shoulder, he drank and offered it to her.

It was eagerly accepted. She had swallowed two large gulps before she realized what it was.

"That should bolster you," Martin grinned, taking the flask from her hand, watching her splutter and cough from the brandy. "Remember," he cautioned, "that I did not invite you to come." When she rose stiffly and limped forward, he relented. "There should be a road near here. It will make walking easier." *And more dangerous*, he added mentally.

They reached the road after a few minutes, and Martin strode on ahead, his pace undaunted while Elizabeth's limp became more pronounced. The beauty of the surrounding countryside was lost on her as she put all her determination towards following his lead and bolstering her spirits with the thought that her brother's plight was far worse than her own.

Running steps brought Elizabeth's eyes from the

ground. She halted and watched in questioning wonder as Martin sprinted towards her, not slowing as he approached.

He hit her with his full weight, hurling them both from the road and down an incline. Rolling over and over, they ended beneath a screen of weeds and bramble. The breath was knocked from Elizabeth in the fall, preventing any protest, and before she could recover her voice, Martin clamped his hand tightly across her mouth while his body pinned her to the ground.

Diverse questions careened through her mind as she thought to understand his sudden madness. The steady tramp of many feet sounded in the distance, then ever closer. Small clouds of dust slowly drifted where they lay hidden as a regiment of French regulars marched by, their baggage train following them.

Martin removed his hand from her mouth as soon as he saw that she understood. When the sounds of the baggage carts faded, he eased from Elizabeth's side until only his arm lay across her chest.

"Would it not be safe to go on now?" she whispered, swallowing hard as she felt the beat of his pulse.

Turning to gaze at her, desire flickered in Martin's eyes.

"We had better move on." Elizabeth tried to raise her hand to remove his arm, a sudden fear entering her heart. "No," she protested as he drew closer. "Don't . . ." Her words were ended by his lips, closing savagely on hers, his arms crushing her to his taut body.

The intensity of his emotion overwhelmed her. Elizabeth felt an answering response well in the depths of her being. It pressed her to surrender to the demands of his lips. As she was on the verge of yielding, a vision of Cavilon exploded in Elizabeth's mind. She erupted into a writhing mass, hitting and clawing at Martin.

He released his hold as if struck by shot and watched her scramble frantically from him, sobs breaking loose when she reached the road. "Oh, God," he swore at himself, then rose and followed. Reaching the road, he saw Elizabeth a little way ahead, trying to compose herself.

That she could not escape the man had come to her as soon as the worst of the panic had passed. She was at his mercy in a strange and hostile land. Elizabeth awaited him. The price of her brother's freedom had suddenly become very dear.

"That will not happen again," Martin said, no regret showing on his impassive face. "We must reach Treguier by nightfall, and there are several miles yet to be gone." He motioned for her to walk on. "I'll get them," he told her when she began to walk back to find their bags. "Go on."

Turning, she walked as briskly as she could, the tiredness, the aches and pains of her protesting body forgotten in the clamour of her thoughts, in the confusion of her heart.

Chapter XX

Darkness had fallen by the time Martin and Elizabeth saw the village of Treguier before them. Each step had become a self-willed process for Elizabeth through the endless day, and she did not protest when Martin told her to hide beneath some low shrubs while he went ahead and found lodging.

Returning an hour later, he found her fast asleep. "*Ma petite*," he murmured, gently picking her up. The comte smiled tiredly as he shifted her weight in his arms. "Mayhaps I have named you wrongly," he quipped, unable to resist the tease, even though she could not hear it. His long strides brought them to a small, neat cottage at the end of a lane on the out- hurriedly about and slipped in when it opened.

"This is the one you spoke of?" the handsome woman asked in surprise as she followed Martin up skirts. Tapping at the door with his boot, he glanced the stairs to a bedchamber. "Your tastes have changed, *mon cher*."

"It is not as you think, Marie-Thérèse." Martin frowned at her. "I have explained it all." He deposited Elizabeth on the bed.

207

"Ah, *oui*," she agreed skeptically, the gentleness with which he removed the sleeping figure's boots reinforcing her own belief. "What ever happened to her?" she asked, her eyes on Elizabeth's dirt-stained face and clothing.

Martin ignored her words and took her arm, guiding her into the corridor outside the bedchamber. "Let her sleep as long as possible. When she awakens, tell her I have gone to learn what I can of her brother and will return as soon as possible. Do not let her go out or be seen by anyone," he cautioned.

"I am suddenly become the fool?" Marie-Thérèse laughed gently. "You had best turn your mind to what you must do or you shall not return," she warned.

"You know what to do if that should happen?"

"It shall not."

Taking her hand, Martin kissed it. "I appreciate this very much."

"Then begone before Monsieur Truval arrives," Marie-Thérèse laughed. "He might not believe you are only an old friend, and I would dislike you having to kill him," she teased, cocking her head coquettishly.

"That would be most incommodious," he agreed with a grin, "not only for you but also for me. I have no wish to explain my presence to a *gendarme*, as you well know. There is no need to show me the way out. I know it."

"One never could keep you from going," she sighed, watching his back disappear down the stairs. Going back into the bedchamber where Elizabeth lay, Marie-Thérèse picked up the candle at the bedside and studied the disheveled, begrimed figure. "I have never before seen that look in Martin's eye when it came to a woman. Not in all the years I have known him." She shook her head. "There is no telling what attracts a man."

Consciousness crept upon Elizabeth in degrees of pain. Not sure why every muscle was aching, she thought to call Spense and opened her eyes. Tiny-figured wallpaper blurred before her. The shoulder which had struck the ground when Martin had tackled her protested vehemently when she tried to sit up. She passed a hand over her eyes and opened them once again. The sight of her reddened, dirt-stained hands brought the memory of the day crashing down upon her.

Where am I? she questioned frantically, gazing about the chamber. The style of the furniture and the delicate papering clearly bespoke the French influence. Where could she be?

Let me think. We were near Treguier, outside it in fact. I hid. Further searching of her mind revealed nothing else. *Did Martin bring me here or did someone find me?* rose the alarming question. Elizabeth struggled upright, threw back the light covering, and saw that she was still fully clothed.

"*Bonjour, mademoiselle.*"

The light, tinkling voice startled Elizabeth. Her eyes swung to the doorway and encountered a vision in a silk negligee.

"But do not be afraid." The ethereal figure floated forward.

"Where . . ." Elizabeth swallowed the lump of fear in her throat. "Where am I? How did I come here?"

"You are in Treguier, *naturellement*. Martin brought you here last night."

The two women eyed each other assessingly, and Elizabeth felt herself defeated at every comparison.

"Where is Martin?" she asked at last.

"Martin." The name rolled off the other's tongue with an intimacy that surprised Elizabeth. "He asked me to tell you he is seeking word of your brother and will return."

"And you . . . ?"

"I am, let us say, an old friend. Allowing you to remain here is a way of repaying a debt," Marie-Thérèse explained as she toyed with the ruffling of her negligee.

"Would it be possible . . . could I not wash?" Elizabeth had suddenly become overwhelmingly aware of the state of her disarray. She swung her feet to the floor and rose stiffly.

"I thought you might wish this." Marie-Thérèse fluttered her hands. "Come, a bath has been prepared." She floated from the room, the silk swirling about her delicate ankles.

Following with a painful limp, Elizabeth found herself wondering if Martin had ever kissed this woman as he had her. She was angered to find she cared what the answer would be.

The luxury of soaking in the warm water, softly perfumed with rose hips, soon revived Elizabeth's spirits and, with their return, curiosity surged strongly.

When Marie-Thérèse returned with a delicately flowered robe of fine cambric, she wrapped it about herself and began seeking answers to some of the questions teeming in her mind. "You say you are an old friend of Martin's?"

"*Oui*, and you?" Marie-Thérèse interrogated in return.

"Oh, no. I did not meet him until two nights past. He has been hired by . . . by a friend to help in bringing my brother home." The other's arch smile made her want to enlarge on the explanation. "I wished to come with him to help. My brother is very ill and requires nursing."

"If he is in one of Bonaparte's prison's, he will require more than that." Marie-Thérèse's features suddenly saddened.

"Why do you think he is in a prison?" Elizabeth countered, wondering what explanation Martin had given her.

"There can be no doubt you are *anglaise*," Marie-Thérèse stated flatly, motioning at her soiled garb on the floor. "I had not thought you English women so daring. Is it perhaps a lover Martin is to free?"

"Of course not," came the immediate, indignant reply. "But I doubt I would have come," she looked down at her painful hands, "if I had known what lay before me."

"But traveling with Martin is its own reward, *n'est-ce pas?*" The French woman winked.

Red flamed to Elizabeth's cheeks. "I don't know what you mean," she choked out.

211

"That I do not believe." Marie-Thérèse's laugh tinkled gaily. "But it is none of my concern. Martin and I are old friends. We ask no questions.

"Now come with me," she continued. "You look to be Margot's size. She left some of her gowns here when she left with that handsome captain last month."

"You live here with other ladies?" Elizabeth asked. "Is this not your home?"

"*Oui*. But living alone does not suit me. There are a few other . . . ladies who stay from time to time." Marie-Thérèse glanced back at her questioningly. Did the English woman not know . . .

"I do hope my presence does not put you in any danger?" Her guest's words broke into her thoughts.

"Not if no one sees you. Here is Margot's room. I will bring a breakfast tray for you. Monsieur Treval always insists I eat with him before he leaves." Marie-Thérèse opened the door and fluttered on her way as Elizabeth stepped into it.

Going to the wardrobe, she chose the simplest of the flamboyant and rather risqué gowns within it. Even at this, the one she chose was so décolleté it made her blush. She began piecing together the conversation she had had with Marie-Thérèse and all she had seen. Just as the Frenchwoman entered with the breakfast tray, the realization dawned.

"Why are you staring so?" the courtesan laughed, setting the tray upon the table in the room.

"Oh, nothing . . . nothing," Elizabeth stammered, her face blanching. "When do you think Martin will return?" she asked.

"When he has learned what he wishes to know. Now

come and eat. You look rather ill at the moment. That gown is quite nice on you. Martin will be pleased."

"But I don't want him to be pleased." Elizabeth's hand went to the low neckline. "I must have my own clothing back," she demanded.

"As soon as it is dry. I ordered it to be washed," Marie-Thérèse said calmly, studying Elizabeth. "Now eat." She watched as the other woman toyed with her food. The young Englishwoman was acting very peculiarly for one who was in the company of Martin. Could it be he spoke the truth? *"Mon Dieu,"* she gasped, watching Elizabeth meticulously unfold the napkin and place it in her lap. This one was not intimate with him. It was indeed her brother he meant to free.

"Yes? Elizabeth looked up.

"Nothing." Marie-Thérèse fluttered her hands. "I was just thinking that your clothing should not be hung out for all to see," she said and hurried from the room.

During the following three days Elizabeth found her hostess polite, even friendly, but insistent that she spend her time in her room, permitting her to move freely about the house only from midday to the late afternoon hours. To all her questions, Elizabeth received evasive answers, learning only that Martin was well thought of and had a loyal, protective friend in Marie-Thérèse. With little to occupy her time, Elizabeth's concern for her brother grew. She clung to remembrances of him as a refuge from the turmoil that thinking of Cavilon and Martin evoked.

At the end of the third day she and Marie-Thérèse were seated in a small parlour when a French peasant silently appeared before them. Relief filled her when she realized it was Martin. "You have found him?" she questioned eagerly.

"Yes, and no." He nodded a greeting to her while going to Marie-Thérèse and kissing her hand. "I now know which prison but not where he is within it," Martin explained, drawing the Frenchwoman to her feet and putting an arm about her waist, winking at her questioning look.

"When shall you make the attempt to free him?" Elizabeth forced herself to continue, trying to ignore the fact that he was kissing Marie-Thérèse's ear.

"In two . . . three days," he replied nonchalantly.

"Three days. But what shall we do until then?"

Martin's eyes flicked to Elizabeth's, then back to Marie-Thérèse.

Feeling a blush spread warmly over her cheeks, Elizabeth rose. "Is such a delay truly necessary? I would think it dangerous for . . . for all of us to remain here overly long."

"The English mind"—he smiled at the woman in his arms—"is always precise. You are correct, Miss Jeffries." He turned his gaze back to her. "We will leave in the morn, before daybreak. I have found an abandoned cottage where we shall be safe enough."

The thought of being alone with this unsettling man caused Elizabeth to pale, but she raised no objection. "I shall be ready in the morn, then," she told him, walking to the door. "Good eve." She glanced back and hurried out.

Martin dropped his hands from Marie-Thérèse as soon as Elizabeth was out of sight and sank tiredly onto the sofa.

The courtesan walked to the sideboard and poured a glass of brandy. Bringing it to him, she sat beside Martin, a frown upon her lips. "I dislike being used to . . ." Seeing his scowl, her words trailed away. She began again. "It was very naughty of you not to tell me what an innocent Miss Jeffries is," she scolded instead. "She was most embarrassed when she realized what kind of a house you had brought her to."

"I'm surprised she didn't march right out." A smile eased the distress and fatigue marking his features.

"The temper is there but also a great deal of common sense. That is what the English women are noted for, *n'est-ce pas?*" When Martin did not answer, she added, "Elizabeth is very troubled and, I think, not only for her brother. She would not speak of herself, and though she was curious to know about you, she flinched whenever your name was mentioned. What have you done to make her so uneasy?"

"Little . . . Enough."

Marie-Thérèse reached out and began massaging the tense muscles in Martin's neck. "At times," she mused reflectively, "I wonder whom each of you really fear—others or merely yourselves?"

Elizabeth's dreams during the night were haunted by Cavilon and Martin. Both men taunted and teased her in relentless pursuit. Lying awake in the early dark hours, she tried to sort through her confused feelings and realized that she felt an attraction for both men but also a revulsion. *Why compare the two?* she questioned for the hundredth time. *They are such opposites, two opposing extremes.*—Cavilon, at times so foppish, even effeminate, and Martin, always arrogant, conceited, even antagonistic.

Why did he desire her when he seemed to hate her? Marie-Thérèse was much more pleasing to him. He had made that abundantly clear, and she was certainly agreeable.

Elizabeth shook herself. Such thoughts would never do. *When Morton is safely in England, Martin will be gone, never to be seen again, and I will wed Cavilon. For now I must concentrate on helping Morton, in not doing anything that will harm his chances to be freed,* she thought.

"Two days alone with Martin," she breathed, a cold chill running through her. Was it caused by fear or by . . . ? Elizabeth shook her head angrily. "Martin is a means of freeing my brother, nothing more," she whispered aloud.

Chapter XXI

Long before anyone thought to stir in Treguier, Martin knocked at Elizabeth's door and was surprised when it opened and she stood before him, dressed in the French culotte and shirt Marie-Thérèse had given her, her duffel bag in hand, ready to depart. Anger welled within him as she raised her troubled eyes to his. "There is food in the kitchen for you," he said tersely, standing back to let her pass. Following her, he pondered his hostile response. He did not understand it or the resentment he felt even as desire for her surged through him. Inner conflict made him pace impatiently while he waited for Elizabeth to finish eating.

"I can take this with me," she told him, seeing his scowl darken.

"Eat. We shall not be able to have a fire. This may be your last warm meal for a time," Martin answered curtly.

Watching the two. Marie-Thérèse was perplexed by Martin's manner with the Englishwoman. It was apparent he was doing his best to make her dislike, even hate, him, yet she was certain he loved her.

217

Whenever his eyes fell on Elizabeth, a hunger appeared. *Ah, men,* Marie-Thérèse sighed to herself. *Does one ever really know them?*

Elizabeth rose from her chair, gulping the last of her coffee. She grabbed the duffel bag she had set beside the table and went to the door. Glancing back, she saw Martin put his arms about Marie-Thérèse, and she hurried out.

He joined her in a few minutes and, signaling for silence, took her hand in his and led the way. Ducking through alleys and around houses, Martin made his way to a low, sagging building. "Wait," he hissed, disappearing into it. Moments later he reappeared leading two horses.

Thank the Lord for these breeches, Elizabeth thought as she took hold the saddle and put her foot into the stirrup. She struggled awkwardly to heave herself up into the unfamiliar French equipage.

Martin watched for several moments, then took hold of her waist and plopped her into the saddle. Vaulting onto his mount, he motioned for her to follow.

They moved at a slow pace until the last cottage was behind them. With the first rays of the sun shooting over the horizon, Martin spurred forward, leaving Treguier behind them and heading for open country. Periodically throughout the morning he slowed the pace to rest the horses. Elizabeth was thankful that they were no longer walking and querulously thought he was being far more careful of the dumb beasts than he had been of her.

Around noon Martin reined to a halt before a stream and told her they would rest for a short time. He pointedly ignored Elizabeth as she crawled down from the saddle and moved painfully to the stream.

"Is it much farther?" she asked when she had finished drinking, her joy in riding lessened by the aches it produced.

"No, an hour more at most," Martin told her curtly.

"Where is my brother?"

"In the prison in Saint-Brieuc."

"Will there be great danger for us?"

"Us?" he scoffed. "You are going to remain at the cottage. There will be trouble enough without you to worry about."

"I have tried to . . . not to be a nuisance." Elizabeth caught the loaf of bread he tossed her.

"The only way you would not have been is not to have come," Martin told her coldly, anger edging his words.

"You have made your feelings quite clear on that point," she retorted, tearing the loaf in two. "But I am here and I see no reason for you to continue to be so abrasively ungentlemanly about it. Perhaps you have never loved someone enough to take risks for them. How was I to know, other than by being here, that you would do your utmost to free my brother. He means nothing to you," she argued.

"There is no reason to shout. You will do nothing but announce our presence. I hardly think you would wish to explain what you are doing here."

"And would you?"

"It is time we move on." Martin turned his back.

Elizabeth threw the two hunks of bread at him in a fit of anger. They bounced harmlessly off his back and fell to the ground.

A low curse sounded. Martin swung around and glared at her. The proud tilt of her head and her long dark hair cascading about her face in disarray heightened her natural glow and accentuated her dark, flashing eyes. "You try me too far," he breathed. Striding forward, he crushed her to him, his lips descending upon hers with savage demand.

Struggling, Elizabeth found that his strength was too great. She felt she was being pulled into a whirlpool that was sweeping her reason away. The emotions Martin's lips evoked came in surging swells, threatening to drown all thought. Resisting, she felt her will weaken, her spirit respond to his passionate appeal. Certain she must surrender, she was saved as Martin drew back.

His eyes were black pools of desire as he picked her up and carried her from the stream's side to a blanket of grass beneath an aged oak.

A warning clanged in Elizabeth's mind, reading his thought as his lips claimed hers once more. "No," she protested weakly when he laid her down and pressed his body to hers. "No." She tried to twist away from him.

"You do not mean that, Elizabeth." Martin caressed her cheek while his other hand unfastened the buttons on her shirt. "You wish this as much as I," he breathed.

"It should not happen this way." She felt tears well in her eyes. "I do not love you."

"I do not believe that." He moved to kiss her, but she twisted her face away.

"I am not like your Marie-Thérèse," she choked out. "You can have her, any woman. Why must you force me?" Tears began to trickle down her face.

"But I am not. Can you deny that you feel the need, that you do not desire me?" Martin questioned harshly, forcing Elizabeth to look at him.

"Desire is not love," she returned in a hoarse whisper, and he felt himself sicken at what he had almost done.

Martin rose angrily.

Sitting up, Elizabeth wiped the tears in her eyes with the back of her hand. "I . . . I do not understand what I felt, only that it was somehow not right, not here. I must have time to think. We have known each other but a few days . . ."

"Love does not need thought," Martin answered angrily, turning away. He paced a few steps away and turned back. "It is your English prudery that makes you hesitate," he told her. "I shall not press you now, but think on it." He came back and took her hand, drawing her up. "You will see that your need is as great as mine."

A whinny sounded in the distance.

"We must go." He pulled her towards the horses. After helping her into the saddle, he vaulted into his own and, spurring, led the way once more.

* * *

Dusting the backless chair in the deserted cottage, Elizabeth sat down, glad to have some time for reflection while Martin went to finish his arrangements for the rescue. So much had happened to her in so short a time that she found it difficult to focus on her brother's plight amidst her turmoil.

I am certain he shall be rescued, Elizabeth thought. *Martin will not fail.* She had no doubt in his ability; her confidence in him was complete. If it could be done, it would be.

But what of yourself? she asked. *What shall you do?* The absorbing response to Martin's passionate embrace had evoked but a promise of what could be, she realized, and it seemed to lend credence to his words. Why should you not surrender yourself to him? an inner voice prompted. Why not grab at this chance, experience the fullness of passion. Do you think the Comte de Cavilon will ever thrill you as this man does?

"Cavilon," Elizabeth murmured. He had said that ardour was tiresome. Indeed, in all his protestations of love, she had seen no hint of ungentlemanly passion. And yet, she thought, there were moments when something lingered in his gaze, when she had thought he would say . . . do . . . more. There had been a tenderness in his gaze, in his gentle kisses that had not left her unmoved. She had thought she hated him, had sworn she despised him, and yet . . .

Can he ever compare to Martin, ever move you as this man can? the voice returned.

But desire is not love, Elizabeth told herself. The words she had uttered so boldly to Martin were no longer convincing. *If I loved either, would these questions plague me?* she asked herself. *You have promised to wed Cavilon,* her conscience told her, entering the fray. *Will you not keep your word? Could there not be affection between you in time?*

But you don't have time, Elizabeth reminded herself. And Martin was so much more a man.

Riding from Saint-Brieuc, Martin felt his excitement grow, as it always did when he was about to dare fate. His plans had been altered by what he had learned. It would not be in two days, but this night. Learning that new guards had arrived early this afternoon at the prison had changed everything. Even now the guards, old and new, were drinking deeply, using the arrival as an excuse to celebrate. Many would never reach their posts, and those who did were not likely to care what was happening. Better to act this night than on the next, when thick heads would make them suspicious of any noise.

Martin was certain that his new plans would please Elizabeth, for she must now take part in the venture. Thoughts of her stirred a feeling deep within him. Had Cavilon lost?

Throwing back his head, a harsh laugh escaped his lips. "Have you become two men instead of one?" he questioned aloud. "Which are you?"

Do you even know anymore? Has the game gone on so long that you have forgotten what and who you truly are? What has happened? His troubled thoughts ran freely. *In seeking identities that could never be connected, or even vaguely suspected as being one, have you gone too far? Why this preoccupation, this insistence that Elizabeth choose between the two? Are you not one man?* He shook his head.

Why does Cavilon tease her while Martin attacks? Why the anger? Answers eluded him.

He laughed softly at himself. It mattered not, perhaps. Martin, it appeared, would triumph. His stomach knotted at the thought, and Rosamon sprang to mind unbidden. She had had a choice between himself and a wealthy weakling and had chosen the latter. Since that time he had never given away his heart. Martin had broken many. Through the years it had always seemed that women chose the stronger or the richer. How much easier it always seemed for them to choose strength, especially if attached to wealth. How much greater must a woman's love be to accept a man's weaknesses and love him in spite of them.

Chapter XXII

"Elizabeth," Martin whispered as he stole into the cottage.

"Here," she answered, rising.

He stepped towards the sound of her voice, and his hand met hers. Martin drew her to him and felt her reluctance. "I have news which shall please you. Your brother shall be free this night."

"You are certain he still lives?" she asked, excitement and fear mingling at his words. "Can it really be?"

With his arm about her waist, Martin guided her out into the moonlit night. "I cannot say for a certainty that he lives, but his name is on the prison manifest. It is more a feeling, of knowing it. I have survived many years through much danger with my instinct alone to perserve me. It does not lead me astray now," he assured her. "The Captain Paraton whom Cavilon spoke of is also listed. I was told to bring him out if I could. In truth, I may need his aid if your brother is as ill as is said. But," he placed his hands on her shoulders, "I shall need your help also."

"I will do anything," she answered fervently.

"Anything?" he felt compelled to tease.

Something in his tone struck Elizabeth as oddly familiar and yet not of his usual mien.

Martin saw the question. He quickly pulled her to him and kissed her. "For luck," he laughed, dropping his hands and taking hold of hers. "Come." His love for the adventure sounded in his word, showed on his features.

"The Lord preserve us," she murmured as he drew her towards the horses. *Oh, I do hope you have enough courage for both of us,* she thought as Martin helped her mount. Riding through the darkness, Elizabeth fought the stomach-churning fear that threatened to overwhelm her.

Signaling for her to rein in beside him when the lights of Saint-Brieuc appeared before them, Martin drew a ragged cloak from behind his saddle. "Put this on," he ordered. "We don't want to have to explain that English complexion. Whatever happens, keep your eyes downcast. Don't look directly at anyone, and stay close to me." When the cloak was securely fastened, he urged his mount forward.

Elizabeth felt a new wonder at his calmness as they rode through the streets of the city. He was leisurely riding, the place well known to him, showing no fear. *Surely this is too daring?* she questioned as they passed other riders and moved around carriages and coach, which she could have touched had she wished. Her heart sank when Martin turned into a small inn's courtyard.

"Ah, monsieur, you have returned." A thin man with an apron about his flat stomach took hold of Martin's reins as he dismounted.

"*Oui.* Do you have everything in readiness?" Martin asked, signaling Elizabeth to dismount.

"Then you are going ahead as planned?"

"*Oui.* Our brother still lives. God grant he will yet see our parents. But we shall not be able to halt until well out of the city, so we shall not return as I thought. They fear the disease will spread." Martin spoke in tones of hushed confidence. "The cart?"

"Just as you wished, and the team is the best I could find on such short notice." The innkeeper's tone matched his. "But they are *très cher* in these times. Napoleon takes all our good horses for the army."

"Let me see the pair. Wait here," Martin instructed Elizabeth.

The innkeeper handed her the reins he held and led Martin into the stable wing of the courtyard. Several people came and went before the two emerged, leading an aged, swaybacked team pulling a rickety two-wheeled cart. That both men looked very pleased amazed Elizabeth, who could see no use in the beasts or vehicle.

"Tie our horses to the cart," Martin ordered her, climbing onto the wooden plank that served as a seat. "Come along." He motioned for her to join him when she had finished.

"What can you mean to do with these dispirited beasts? They could not go fast enough to evade a child, much less soldiers."

"Français," Martin spat. "Until we are out of the city you must speak only French," he continued, taking his own advice.

Elizabeth marveled at his accent just as she had when he had spoken with the innkeeper. She had taken him to be an Englishman, but his French was that of a native. *There is so much I don't know about this man,* she thought. "Why do we stop here?" she asked a short time later, looking about the narrow alley they had entered. There was nothing in sight that she could see would be of aid to them on this night. Taking the reins Martin handed her, Elizabeth watched him untie their mounts and lead them through an open door into what she had thought to be a house. "Why did you do that? Where have you taken them?" she asked when he returned.

"Where they shall safely await us. The family owes me a favour. If we left the horses tied on the street, they would have been stolen before we had time to turn about. We shall reach the prison soon. Remember to do as I say."

"Would it not help if I knew what was going to happen?"

"It is a very simple plan. We are going to collect our brother who has taken the pox," Martin told her. "Do not speak with anyone . . . your accent would betray us."

Excitement grew as they jostled through the streets. Fear tightened a band about Elizabeth's heart. She saw the prison loom before them.

"Arrêtez!" One of the guards barred their way at the entrance.

Smoke from the oil-soaked torches standing about the arched entry caused Elizabeth to choke and cough as a breeze wafted it across the cart.

"What is your business?" a second guard demanded, swaggering to the cart's side.

Martin handed a crumpled piece of paper to him. "We be told by the priest in our village that this says we must come and take our brother home. That he has taken the pox," he whined, bobbing a bow. "And Jacques here be sick also."

"You may enter." The guard motioned the one before the cart to move aside after the briefest of glances at the paper.

"Where be he found?" Martin asked as the two men returned to the jugs of wine by the wall.

"You'll find someone who can tell you where he is in the right corner of the quadrangle. Don't bother stopping when you leave," he snarled, raising the bottle to his lips.

"*Oui.*" Martin bobbed another hasty bow and flicked the reins. Halting the cart in the far right corner of the quadrangle, he jumped down and tied the team, then motioned for Elizabeth to follow. All about the open courtyard in the inner colonnade, parties of off-duty guards and their women drank and danced. Some were sprawled about in drunken sleep, others sat gambling and drinking. Picking their way through these, Martin led Elizabeth to an office where a guard sat with his head upon the desk, snoring loudly.

"Stay here," Martin whispered. "Let me know if anyone comes." Stealing to the desk, he began rifling through the papers on it and then through the drawers. A smile came as he found a listing of prisoners. Halfway through the second page he found young Jeffries' name. Noting the section of the prison he was in, Martin returned the papers to the drawer. "Let's go." He brushed past Elizabeth.

She ran after him, following as he wended through corridors and finally down a series of stairs to ever deeper levels. Smokey torches provided the only light in the damp, stench-ridden corridors. Elizabeth shivered as moans and groans filled the air.

"*Arrêtez!*" The guard's voice froze her in her steps. Daring to peer around Martin's back, she saw an iron gate. Two men stood before it.

"We be told to fetch the body of a man called Jeffries," Martin told them, his hands twisting nervously as he bowed. "They said to give ye this." He fumbled in his coat and withdrew a glass bottle, holding it forth with a shaking hand.

"When was ye told there was a body?" one of the guard's demanded, grabbing the bottle.

" 'Twas early in the morn, but we had many bodies ta take up. The pox be bad again." Martin shrugged worriedly.

"Go ahead. Next time come when word is sent. The guard at the end of the corridor to the right will know where the body be. These English aren't proving very hardy." He laughed.

Martin shuffled forward with Elizabeth doing likewise, keeping her eyes fast on the foul, straw-strewn stones.

Repeating the same tale, Martin gave out another

bottle to the next guard, and waited while he thumbed through a grimy, smeared sheaf of papers.

The man grunted and picked up the huge ring of keys on his desk. "Ye be in luck I ken read," he told them. "Else ye'd 'ave ta search through all the cells till ye found 'im." Halting before a door, he unlocked it and pushed it open. "Ye go 'n find 'im."

They ducked through the doorway and waited for their eyes to adjust to the darkness. Elizabeth gagged as the stench overcame her and the horror of the dank, dark open room confronted her. Rats scurried away as they walked forward. All about them prisoners were sprawled in their own wastes. Rotting and putrid flesh mingled in common.

"Steady." Martin's hand gripped Elizabeth's arm as she swayed. He drew her forward, taking the smoking torch from the center column, and began working through the prone forms of what had once been proud soldiers and sailors.

"He cannot be here." Elizabeth shrank from the sight and smell.

"We won't know if you don't look," Martin's cold voice stiffened her.

Clenching her fists, she followed his steps. "Morton," she called out softly. "Morton Jeffries."

A wiry figure rose from the shadows. "Who are you?" the bearded scarecrow questioned.

"You cannot be Morton," Elizabeth gasped, looking at the tattered form with the large, deeply sunken eyes.

"No, I am Captain James Paraton. Jeffries is back here." He motioned behind him.

Stepping in that direction, Martin waved the torch until he located the emaciated figure lying on a heap of befouled straw.

"Morton," Elizabeth said softly, easing past Martin. "Morton Jeffries?"

The man nodded weakly.

"Oh, God," she moaned, laying a hand on his feverish forehead.

"I've done what I could for him," Captain Paraton told Martin. "Who are you? Why have you come?"

"Never mind who we are." Martin handed the torch to him. Kneeling beside Morton, he drew a slim case from his coat. With swift motions he opened the jars within it and expertly applied their contents to Morton's hands, chest, and face.

"What are you doing?" Elizabeth stared at him.

"He has the pox, remember? We must make him look it." Finished, he closed the jars, put them in the case, and returned it to his jacket. "Are you strong enough to help carry him?" he asked the captain.

"Yes."

"Is there another officer here? Get him," Martin commanded.

"This is Captain Herrick." Paraton brought a man forward. "He's only been here three months."

"Listen closely, Captain. I am taking Jeffries and Paraton with me. Wait for a half hour, then all who are able can make a try for freedom. Agree to this or I'll see the door is locked when we go."

"Why shouldn't we all go now?"

"Because then none of us would have a chance. The alarm would be raised before we reached the air. The way I suggest means that some of you will make it. They think we are removing a dead man and are not suspicious. There are only two guards on the gate at the corridor, and I will take care of them. Most of the others are drunk. Let us get away. Jeffries has no chance if we have to fight our way out," Martin said persuasively.

"A half hour and no more," Herrick agreed. "But how am I to know when it is past?"

"Here is a timepiece." Martin placed it in his hand. "Good fortune be yours."

"And to all of you," Herrick returned, shaking his hand.

Motioning for Elizabeth and Paraton to carry Morton, Martin went to the door and pounded on it. "Let us out," he called. "We've found him," he told the guard when the door opened. Stepping out, he sprang at the man, his arm going about his throat. Martin slammed the guard's head against the stone wall and let him fall to the floor. "Lay him down," he whispered, closing the door when the others were out. "Help me." Paraton and Martin began stripping the clothes from the unconscious figure. "Put them on," he instructed the captain as he tied the guard's hands and feet.

Waiting until this was done, he ordered, "Go straight down the center of the corridor. I'll follow right behind you." He picked up the man's short sword.

Elizabeth could hear her heart pounding in her ears as they approached the security gate. One of the guards turned the key and opened it. She walked forward and kept going even when she heard one exclaim, "What's this?" The clang of sword against sword echoed in the corridor.

"Let's stop," Paraton told her. "I must help him."

Glancing back, Elizabeth saw Martin fighting fiercely with the two men. She took in the awful smile that covered his features. *Why, he enjoys this*, she realized, shocked.

One guard fell, cut down by the sword; the other backed away, fear gripping him. It was no match, and he also fell.

A dreamlike state descended over Elizabeth as Martin rushed forward, the bloodied sword in his hand. "Hurry," he urged.

Somehow they made their way back to the cart. Everything seemed unreal as Martin had Paraton lie in the cart. They laid Morton atop him. Then she was on the plank beside him and they were driving through the gate, then moving through the city. Once outside it, they substituted the worn-out nags for sound horses, setting the former free. By dawn they had returned to the abandoned cottage.

After hiding the cart and horses, Martin returned to the cottage and came to the pallet where Morton lay. "How does he fare?" he asked Elizabeth.

"He is very weak, nearly starved to death. Captain Paraton was right about his having a putrid infection of the lungs."

Morton groaned and went into a fit of coughing.

"We must get him someplace where we can find the food he needs, the proper medicines. It will take more than the simple powders I have brought. The skill I have is far too little to save him," Elizabeth said, lifting her eyes to his.

"Give him this," he told her, handing over the flask of brandy. "We go on as soon as it is dark." Martin looked from her to Captain Paraton. "It will be a hard journey, rough and fast, but there is no help for it. They are certain to be out searching," he explained. "I will watch him, Elizabeth. Try to sleep for a time. You will need your strength."

Chapter XXIII

The sloop rode gently on the waves as the dinghy neared it. Morton Jeffries was taken aboard and Elizabeth, Paraton, and Martin scrambled up the rope ladder. After answering Barney's eager greeting, Elizabeth hurried after her brother, who had been carried to the captain's cabin.

"Welcome aboard," Captain Hattern greeted his friend, then shouted orders, getting the sloop under sail.

"Glad to be here," Martin grinned. "This is Captain Paraton—of the king's army, despite his present uniform," he introduced the thin, bearded figure at his side.

"You don't know how glad I am to be on an English ship," Paraton said as the two shook hands.

"The captain could use some hot food and rest," Martin said. "And I imagine he wouldn't mind a sailor's suit."

"Jud," Hattern shouted, "take Captain Paraton below and see to 'is needs. Ye can sleep when ye're done, cap'n. We'll wake ye when we come ta port."

"Thank you." The captain shook his hand again.

"And you." He turned to Martin, then followed the sailor.

"Have you brought the doctor?" Martin asked.

"Just as ye ordered," the craggy captain answered. "How be the lad?"

"Poor at best. The journey to the coast didn't help, but at least we had no trouble. I was surprised there weren't more soldiers out searching."

"'Aven't ye 'eard? Bonaparte's retaken northern Italy. All the troops that could be spared were with 'im, and now most go to Paris for a jubilee, but they say over five thousand Frenchmen lie dead on the Marengo plain."

"When did this happen?"

"A month past by now. Mid-June it were. Bonaparte returned to Paris on the first or second of this month, from what we 'ave 'eard."

"No doubt hailed the hero." Martin shook his head. "How many more Frenchmen will die before the man is satisfied?" He looked across the water at the disappearing land.

"Strange words, Martin. What of we Englishmen? The lad below?"

"What of men? They die no matter what they are called. Come." He clapped Hattern on the back. "I need a cup of your hot grog."

"It'll please ye ta know Lord Fromby was unpleasantly surprised by the excise men yester morn. 'Appened ta meet a 'friend' this afternoon afore we made our way here," Hattern explained. "The bloody fool actually went out on 'is ship fer the run."

A slow smile spread across Martin's lips. "Let us

hope the doctor's words on young Jeffries are as pleasing as your news."

Elizabeth leaned on the railing of the sloop, gazing at the moon's reflection on the low waves.

"It is beautiful, is it not?"

"Yes," she answered, not needing to turn to know that Martin stood beside her.

"I am glad to hear your brother's life is not likely to be forfeited."

"But he is very seriously ill. The doctor says it will take careful nursing if he is to mend. I . . . I cannot find words which adequately express my . . . gratitude for what you have done."

"You needn't say anything." Martin put his arm about her waist and turned her to face him. "Your brother is safe now, and there is nothing for you to think of but us."

Shaking her head, Elizabeth put her fingers to his lips. "I have thought much of . . . us, of you. I do not deny that you have the power to move me, to move me more deeply than I ever thought possible. No, listen to me first," Elizabeth asked as his arms tightened about her, his head bent down.

Martin eased his hold, and she turned towards the sea. "We have little in common, we two," she began after a pause. "And we know little of one another. I dare not question you about the work you do, for fear of what the answers would be. I do know you enjoy the excitement of danger. . . . I saw that in the prison corridor when you fought those guards."

"I do not relish killing," Martin told her tonelessly.

"Oh, I don't think you do, but you do enjoy the challenge of battle, of having your strength tested."

"And what is wrong in that?" he demanded.

"Nothing in itself." Elizabeth turned to him. "It is just that I am an ordinary woman who wants the ordinary things in life. I cannot see you settling for that."

"But we need not settle for that." Martin drew her to him.

"How long would this passion last? How long has your desire for any one woman lasted?" She searched his face questioningly.

"You cannot expect that I have lived like a monk . . ."

"No. That there have been others is not what troubles me."

"Then come to me. Let me teach you what love really is." His hands gripped her shoulders.

"I am not free to come."

"Who is to stop you?" he laughed, his hands sliding down her back, drawing her closer. "Show him to me and he will trouble you no longer."

"I have no doubt he would tremble before you," Elizabeth said sadly.

"Then nothing stops you." Martin drew her to him and claimed her lips in a passionate appeal.

The coil of desire began to stir in Elizabeth as his lips moved insistently against hers. Resolve weakened, began to crumble.

Martin felt the beginning of her response and drew back in anger, half-disguised as passion. "See," he breathed heavily, "together we could go to such heights. I will show you what it is to be loved."

The last gleam of hesitance he saw in her eyes spurred his words. "We shall go anywhere you desire. I am rich. There are no bounds to what we can do. Why are you afraid? With me you need never fear."

"I must return to my brother." She retreated inwardly and tried to move away from him.

"No. I will have an answer," he demanded.

"My word has been given to another."

"If you were released, would you come to me?"

"I . . . I don't know."

"Then go to this man. Tell him you love me," Martin urged.

"Honour binds me to speak of you, but he may still hold me bound to him," Elizabeth told him, looking unflinchingly into his dark, glittering eyes. "Why do you look at me so strangely?" She raised a hand to his cheek.

"You will speak to him?"

"First I must see my brother's health returned. Then I shall. Tell me where I can write you. I cannot promise to come."

"Can you not say you love me?"

She shook her head. "I play no game with you. I don't understand myself why there is this doubt." Elizabeth laid a hand on his arm, imploring him to understand, but he looked away. "There is a lack . . . something which I must resolve before I am free to do anything."

"I have never waited for a woman to choose me," Martin told her coldly."But . . . I do love you. When you have decided, send a letter to Captain Hattern. He will see it reaches me."

Elizabeth nodded.

"Farewell, my love. You shall not see me again unless you send word I may come for you." Martin crushed her to him, kissing her with an ardour that flamed her passion to life. Releasing her as suddenly as he had embraced her, he strode silently away.

Wrapping her arms about herself to still a pounding heart, Elizabeth stifled the urge to cry out and hurried back to her brother.

"It pleases me greatly that you consented to bring Morton here," Sir Henry told Elizabeth as they walked in the garden.

"To be truthful, Uncle, Morton insisted upon coming. He is much improved in the past month."

"The lad has more sense than I've given him," Sir Henry noted. "Nursing him yourself has been too much for you, too great a burden. Look how worn you've become. Why, you're as thin as I am," he scolded.

They walked on for a time in silence, each with his own thoughts.

"Have you seen the Comte de Cavilon since your return to England?" Sir Henry asked.

"No. He has written inquiring about Morton and said he would take care of any expenses. He has sent me flowers each week, but I have not seen him." Elizabeth kept her eyes on the roses they were walking past. A few steps farther on she halted suddenly and turned to her uncle. "When you wed Aunt Lettie, were you passionately in love with her?"

"What an indelicate question, my dear," Sir Henry

noted in surprise, a scowl coming to his features to hide his embarrassment.

"Uncle Henry, if you will not speak with me, who shall?" Elizabeth implored him.

He looked at her keenly, then took her arm. "All right, my dear, I shall answer what I can. Let us continue our walk."

"Did you feel . . . ardour . . . the need for Aunt Lettie . . . for anyone before you wed?" she repeated.

"There were one or two who . . . well, who stirred me so to speak. Poets use such terms." He laughed softly, keeping his eyes straight before him as they walked. "But that was a matter of desire, need, if you will. Now, my Lettie, she was a proper lady and never permitted me more than a kiss or two before we wed. Of course her harridan of a mother, who never left us alone for more than a second, could have been the cause of that. But to your question. No, she did not fill me with passionate longing. It was more a feeling she gave me when I heard the sound of her voice before she came into a room She knew how to tease me out of an ill humour . . . and so many small things I never realized until she was gone. No, Elizabeth, I did not wed your aunt in a blaze of passion, but that does not mean it did not burn brightly for us. " His voice become thick with emotion. "Mayhaps it was more vivid because it grew with us and was not a mere flash, which once experienced is gone.

"But for others the reverse is oft true," he continued thoughtfully. "Each one of us must make his own way. Happiness in never guaranteed."

"I know, Uncle."

"Elizabeth!" Suzanne Chatworth's voice sounded from the house. "Where are you?"

"Coming," she answered. Reaching up, she brushed her uncle's cheek with a kiss and ran towards the house. "How good to see you, Suzanne," she returned the younger woman's greeting hug.

"My goodness, Elizabeth, how thin you've become," she explaimed. "I hope it does not mean Morton has not grown better? How does he fare?"

"Improving more each day. In fact, I think a visitor is just what he needs. Come along." She took Suzanne's arm in her own. "Morton has asked about your family several times since we arrived two days ago. In fact, he asked after you while we were in Folkestone."

A red tinge came to Suzanne's cheeks. "How kind of him," she murmured.

"The day of your summer party . . . do you remember it?" Elizabeth questioned as they walked up the stairs.

"Of course."

"Why did you flirt so outrageously with the Comte de Cavilon?" she paused at the top of the stairs.

"I . . ."

"The truth."

"I was trying to help you, to make you see you could become jealous," Suzanne began , lowering her eyes. "Your Aunt Waddie had said it was you he offered . . ."

"You needn't explain." Elizabeth smiled and walked on. "Wait just a moment," she instructed, halting before the first door they came to. Knocking, she entered. "You can go in," she smiled after glancing in. "I shall be in the garden."

"Thank you." Suzanne hugged her and hastened inside.

Elizabeth took one backward glance at the embracing lovers and pulled the door shut. *How blind I was,* she thought, going to the stairs, *not to have seen what was plainly before me. But I have learned much, and it is time my own decision was made.*

A week later, having been informed of the Comte de Cavilon's arrival, Elizabeth approached the open doors of the salon slowly. She halted a short distance from them.

"My felicitations on your nephew's betrothal," she heard the comte's voice say. "His continuing recovery must be a pleasure to you."

Elizabeth's brow furrowed. The voice struck a strange note of familiarity. Shrugging it aside, she walked in.

"Elizabeth, we meet again at last." Cavilon rose and bowed with a flourish. Coming to her side, he kissed her hand.

"I will leave you," Sir Henry told them and hurried out, closing the doors behind him.

"I suppose this *is* proper." Cavilon drew his lacy kerchief from his waistcoat and sniffed into it daintily. "We are betrothed, *n'est-ce pas?*"

"There is a pledge between us," Elizabeth answered, studying him closely, that same feeling of recognition she had felt earlier returning. "How is Tom? And, of course, Barney?"

"I believe both are well. The lad is very good with horses. You know," he raised an eyebrow, "I never did understand what occurred. Why was it you were not in Folkestone when my agent arrived with the lad?"

"But we have plenty of time to discuss such a trivial matter." He waved her reply aside. "Please, come and sit, *ma petite*." The comte motioned to a chair. "When shall our betrothal be announced?" He seated himself and leaned back languidly.

"You must hear me out and then decide if you still wish to wed me," Elizabeth told him, folding her hands carefully, and raising her eyes to his. *It is odd,* she thought, *that I never before noticed how dark his eyes are.*

"I await your words." He fluttered his kerchief indifferently.

"When you left Folkestone, I did not remain there, nor did I return her," she told him. "It matters not how, but I went with the man you hired to rescue Morton. Barney was with me also. That is why he could not be found when your agent searched for him," she added, then shook herself. "We traveled together from Fokestone to France, then to Saint-Brieuc and back."

"Alone?" Cavilon's face was impassive. His eyelids had drooped, covering any reaction which might reflect in his eyes.

"Yes. During that time we came to know one another well. Quite well."

"So I would imagine, knowing Martin," Cavilon drawled. "You now wish to be free to go to him?"

"I did not say that. Until a few moments ago I was

245

uncertain what I wished to do. Martin did ask me to come to him."

"Do you . . . love him?"

"He is an attractive man. Handsome, stong. There is a sense of adventure about him that is exciting. It would be very difficult for any woman not to yield to his charms.

Rising, Cavilon sauntered to the window. "And so you too have succumbed to his . . . charms?"

"The desire to do so was very strong," Elizabeth said in a low voice, rising.

"And if I do not release you from your promise, you will go to him anyway?" The comte's voice tightened as if his throat had constricted.

"Do you wish me to?" She stepped towards him.

"You would still wed me?" Cavilon's back remained to her.

"Yes."

"Because of my wealth?" he asked bitterly.

"Martin has assured me he is also wealthy. I have no reason to doubt him."

"Then why? Cavilon turned to her. "Why? Because you gave me your word?"

"Because I believe I love you," Elizabeth answered simply.

"Love me?" he repeated scornfully. "A pitiful fop who is laughed at, derided behind his back. You would have me believe you choose me over a man like this Martin? Do you think I am a fool?"

"You are kind and gentle." Elizabeth laid a hand on his arm. "And only those who have suffered know what it means to be thus."

"And Martin is not?"

"There is a kindness in Martin but it comes only from his strength. He feels the stronger and therefore believes he can afford the luxury of kindness. It adds to his stature. You attempt to hide your kindness. Just as you believe this," she brushed a hand against his powdered cheek, "protects you."

Cavilon stiffened, wondering at the meaning of her words. "And you would think nothing of rejecting Martin?"

"It troubles me that he should be hurt in any way, but I cannot believe the pain will be long or lasting. He is a man who thrives on action and adventure, on women's adoration. There is plenty of both for him. I shall be quickly forgotten."

A wave of strong emotion swept across the comte's face. "You shall never be forgotten," came the deep-voiced words.

Elizabeth stared at him and gasped.

Reaching up, the comte removed the powdered peruke covering his thick black hair.

"It cannot be." she breathed. All the strange glimpses, the odd moments that had seemed so peculiar flashed to mind. "Why would you do such a thing to me?"

"I did not mean for you to meet Martin," Cavilon began. "And when you did, it was as if a demon possessed me. Once, long ago," he tried to explain, "I believed someone loved me, and I was betrayed by that love. All these years I have never loved another, and yet I could not reason my feelings for you away. They kept prodding me on, refusing to let me put them aside in peace."

"I don't understand." Elizabeth shook her head.

"I myself have not fathomed it entirely. I don't know why I acted as I did. I can only ask that you forgive me." His eyes implored her. "Forgive both . . ."

"How easy it would be to rage at you." Elizabeth took several deep breaths, staving off her temper.

"That, I believe, you could do very well, *ma petite*," Cavilon gently teased her.

A smile slowly came to Elizabeth's lips. She laughed softly. "Uncle Henry is a wise man," she sighed. "I fear I am in the sullens too oft for it to be wise to send you away."

Cavilon cocked his head questioningly. Seeing the answer he sought in her eyes, he drew Elizabeth into his arms. Slowly he bent his head to kiss her, first in a gentle pledge, which proved but a spark to the desire rising in both of them.

Sometime later as they sat on the sofa, Elizabeth laid her head against Cavilon's arm and gazed lovingly at him. "Will I truly be a comtesse?" she teased.

"So it does matter," he drawled.

Elizabeth frowned.

"The title is genuine," the comte smiled. "But you shall have to endure my powder and rouge in public for some time to come. It would be dangerous to drop the pose suddenly. I want none of my . . . enemies to take their revenge by harming you."

"Do I dare ask what you have been doing all these years?"

"I have been an agent for the government." Cavilon became very serious. "You shall learn no more than that."

"How many know of you and Martin?"

"Only one. My skill at disguise is not a small talent." He posed affectedly.

"Is that one Lord Tretain?" she guessed shrewdly.

"*Ma chère petite*, we have more interesting matters to discuss." Cavilon took her hand and kissed it, then her wrist.

Elizabeth drew back.

"Adrian knows, but not Juliane." The comte sighed and lifted an eyebrow. "She will be most happy to see me leg-shackled at last."

"How is she?" Elizabeth suddenly remembered her condition.

"A son. Louis. As of the past week." He smiled. "We shall be hard put to match them," he teased.

"You know—" Elizabeth ignored his words and poised a finger on her chin—"this is most interesting. Tell me, how am I to know if you are truly the odd gentleman or the curious rogue?"

"She wounds me," he sighed, then became serious. "The true comte lies somewhere between the two." A teasing smile came to his lips. "But when you look at me like that," his hand caressed her chin, "I definitely prefer Martin's methods."

"There are times when a little of Martin could be interesting," she agreed.

Their mutual smiles altered subtly as they read the desire in each other.

"I love *you*," Elizabeth breathed.

"And I, you." Cavilon's eyes spoke his understanding.

They kissed tenderly, embracing one another.

"Uncle Henry will be concerned if we do not call him soon," she sighed sometime later.

"La," Cavilon drawled the tease, "how am I ever to explain the immediate need of a special license to him?"

"Could it be that you no longer find ardour tiresome, my lord? Elizabeth questioned in mock surprise as Cavilon drew the peruke over his dark mane.

Pausing outside the doors of the salon, Sir Henry heard the question. When no reply sounded, he opened the doors slightly and saw that the answer was definitely not debatable. Smiling broadly, he pulled the door shut and returned to the gardens.

Love—the way you want it!

Candlelight Romances

		TITLE NO.	
☐ A MAN OF HER CHOOSING by Nina Pykare	$1.50	#554	(15133-3)
☐ PASSING FANCY by Mary Linn Roby	$1.50	#555	(16770-1)
☐ THE DEMON COUNT by Anne Stuart	$1.25	#557	(11906-5)
☐ WHERE SHADOWS LINGER by Janis Susan May	$1.25	#556	(19777-5)
☐ OMEN FOR LOVE by Esther Boyd	$1.25	#552	(16108-8)
☐ MAYBE TOMORROW by Marie Pershing	$1.25	#553	(14909-6)
☐ LOVE IN DISGUISE by Nina Pykare	$1.50	#548	(15229-1)
☐ THE RUNAWAY HEIRESS by Lillian Cheatham	$1.50	#549	(18083-X)
☐ HOME TO THE HIGHLANDS by Jessica Eliot	$1.25	#550	(13104-9)
☐ DARK LEGACY by Candace Connell	$1.25	#551	(11771-2)
☐ LEGACY OF THE HEART by Lorena McCourtney	$1.25	#546	(15645-9)
☐ THE SLEEPING HEIRESS by Phyllis Taylor Pianka	$1.50	#543	(17551-8)
☐ DAISY by Jennie Tremaine	$1.50	#542	(11683-X)
☐ RING THE BELL SOFTLY by Margaret James	$1.25	#545	(17626-3)
☐ GUARDIAN OF INNOCENCE by Judy Boynton	$1.25	#544	(11862-X)
☐ THE LONG ENCHANTMENT by Helen Nuelle	$1.25	#540	(15407-3)
☐ SECRET LONGINGS by Nancy Kennedy	$1.25	#541	(17609-3)

At your local bookstore or use this handy coupon for ordering:

Dell DELL BOOKS
P.O. BOX 1000, PINEBROOK, N.J. 07058

Please send me the books I have checked above. I am enclosing $ _____
(please add 75¢ per copy to cover postage and handling). Send check or money order—no cash or C.O.D.'s. Please allow up to 8 weeks for shipment.

Mr/Mrs/Miss _____

Address _____

City _____ State/Zip _____

Once you've tasted joy and passion, do you dare dream of

LOVING

Danielle Steel

bestselling author of
The Promise and *To Love Again*

Bettina Daniels lived in a gilded world—pampered, adored, adoring. She had youth, beauty and a glamorous life that circled the globe—everything her father's love, fame and money could buy. Suddenly, Justin Daniels was gone. Bettina stood alone before a mountain of debts and a world of strangers—men who promised her many things, who tempted her with words of love. But Bettina had to live her own life, seize her own dreams and take her own chances. But could she pay the bittersweet price?

A Dell Book =============================== $2.75 (14684-4)

At your local bookstore or use this handy coupon for ordering:

| Dell | **DELL BOOKS** LOVING $2.75 (14684-4) **P.O. BOX 1000, PINEBROOK, N.J. 07058** |

Please send me the above title. I am enclosing $ _____
(please add 75¢ per copy to cover postage and handling). Send check or money order—no cash or C.O.D.'s. Please allow up to 8 weeks for shipment.

Mr/Mrs/Miss _____

Address _____

City _____ State/Zip _____

THE DARK HORSEMAN

Marianne Harvey
author of *The Proud Hunter*

Beautiful Donna Penroze had sworn to her dying father that she would save her sole legacy, the crumbling tin mines and the ancient, desolate estate *Trencobban*. But the mines were failing, and Donna had no one to turn to. No one except the mysterious Nicholas Trevarvas—rich, arrogant, commanding. Donna would do anything but surrender her pride, anything but admit her irresistible longing for *The Dark Horseman*.

A Dell Book $3.25

At your local bookstore or use this handy coupon for ordering:

Dell | **DELL BOOKS** THE DARK HORSEMAN (11758-5) $3.25
P.O. BOX 1000, PINEBROOK, N.J. 07058

Please send me the above title. I am enclosing $_____
(please add 75¢ per copy to cover postage and handling). Send check or money order—no cash or C.O.D.'s. Please allow up to 8 weeks for shipment.

Mr/Mrs/Miss_____

Address_____

City_____State/Zip_____

The passionate sequel to the scorching novel of fierce pride and forbidden love

THE PROUD HUNTER

by Marianne Harvey

Author of *The Dark Horseman*
and *The Wild One*

Trefyn Connor—he demanded all that was his—and more—with the arrogance of a man who fought to win . . . with the passion of a man who meant to possess his enemy's daughter and make her pay the price!

Juliet Trevarvas—the beautiful daughter of The Dark Horseman. She would make Trefyn come to her. She would taunt him, shock him, claim him body and soul before she would surrender to THE PROUD HUNTER.

A Dell Book $3.25 (17098-2)

At your local bookstore or use this handy coupon for ordering:

| **Dell** | **DELL BOOKS** THE PROUD HUNTER $3.25 (17098-2)
P.O. BOX 1000, PINEBROOK, N.J. 07058 |

Please send me the above title. I am enclosing $ _____
(please add 75¢ per copy to cover postage and handling). Send check or money order—no cash or C.O.D.'s. Please allow up to 8 weeks for shipment.

Mr/Mrs/Miss _____

Address _____

City _____ State/Zip _____

She was born with a woman's passion, a warrior's destiny, and a beauty no man could resist.

Firebrand's Woman

Vanessa Royall

Author of *Flames of Desire* and *Come Faith, Come Fire*

Gyva—a beautiful half-breed cruelly banished from her tribe, she lived as an exile in the white man's alien world.

Firebrand—the legendary Chickasaw chief, he swore to defend his people against the hungry settlers. He also swore to win back Gyva. Together in the face of defeat, they will forge a brave and victorious new dream.

A Dell Book $3.50 (14777-8)

At your local bookstore or use this handy coupon for ordering:

Dell	DELL BOOKS FIREBRAND'S WOMAN $3.50 (14777-8)
	P.O. BOX 1000, PINEBROOK, N.J. 07058

Please send me the above title. I am enclosing $_____
(please add 75¢ per copy to cover postage and handling). Send check or money order—no cash or C.O.D.'s. Please allow up to 8 weeks for shipment.

Mr/Mrs/Miss_____

Address_____

City_____ State/Zip_____

Dell Bestsellers

- [ ] **RANDOM WINDS** by Belva Plain $3.50 (17158-X)
- [ ] **MEN IN LOVE** by Nancy Friday $3.50 (15404-9)
- [ ] **JAILBIRD** by Kurt Vonnegut $3.25 (15447-2)
- [ ] **LOVE: Poems** by Danielle Steel $2.50 (15377-8)
- [ ] **SHOGUN** by James Clavell $3.50 (17800-2)
- [ ] **WILL** by G. Gordon Liddy $3.50 (09666-9)
- [ ] **THE ESTABLISHMENT** by Howard Fast........$3.25 (12296-1)
- [ ] **LIGHT OF LOVE** by Barbara Cartland $2.50 (15402-2)
- [ ] **SERPENTINE** by Thomas Thompson $3.50 (17611-5)
- [ ] **MY MOTHER/MY SELF** by Nancy Friday $3.25 (15663-7)
- [ ] **EVERGREEN** by Belva Plain $3.50 (13278-9)
- [ ] **THE WINDSOR STORY**
  by J. Bryan III & Charles J.V. Murphy $3.75 (19346-X)
- [ ] **THE PROUD HUNTER** by Marianne Harvey ..$3.25 (17098-2)
- [ ] **HIT ME WITH A RAINBOW**
  by James Kirkwood $3.25 (13622-9)
- [ ] **MIDNIGHT MOVIES** by David Kaufelt $2.75 (15728-5)
- [ ] **THE DEBRIEFING** by Robert Litell $2.75 (01873-5)
- [ ] **SHAMAN'S DAUGHTER** by Nan Salerno
  & Rosamond Vanderburgh $3.25 (17863-0)
- [ ] **WOMAN OF TEXAS** by R.T. Stevens $2.95 (19555-1)
- [ ] **DEVIL'S LOVE** by Lane Harris $2.95 (11915-4)

At your local bookstore or use this handy coupon for ordering:

DELL BOOKS
P.O. BOX 1000, PINEBROOK, N.J. 07058

Please send me the books I have checked above. I am enclosing $ _____
(please add 75¢ per copy to cover postage and handling). Send check or money order—no cash or C.O.D.'s. Please allow up to 8 weeks for shipment.

Mr/Mrs/Miss _____

Address _____

City _____ State/Zip _____